CHASING CONNOR

JAYNE KINGSLEY

BLUEBERRY LANE
PUBLISHING

To all those who love to read romance.

Love isn't part of the design, until it is ... Gray Designs is Sydney's premier architectural firm. Family run, they are all about being the best and hiring the best. What the employees don't count on is Brian Gray, founder and informal match-maker meddling in their private lives.

Let the fun begin.

Love by Design series features steamy contemporary office romance. Whilst part of a series, each book can be read as a stand alone.

ABOUT THE AUTHOR

Jayne Kingsley writes contemporary romance filled with fashionable and fun heroines and the hunky heroes that capture their hearts. She currently resides on the picturesque south coast of NSW with her two young daughters and her own real-life gorgeous hero.

She loves connecting with her readers. Head to www.jaynekingsley.com to sign up to her newsletter, or join her official facebook page.

Ava De Vere dug the toe of her scuffed school shoes into the dirt. The black was so faded at the front it was hard to tell they'd once been black anyway, so a little more dirt wouldn't hurt. Her mum wouldn't agree—that was if she even noticed.

Ava snorted. Who was she kidding? Her mum wouldn't notice. The only time her mother noticed anything about Ava was when the monthly parenting allowance didn't turn up, and her mum demanded she call her father to remind him of his obligation.

The whole situation sucked big time.

But not as much as today was going to suck if she didn't pay Julie and her gang back the money she'd borrowed from them. Julie sucked. Her gang sucked. School *really* sucked.

For good measure, she dug the toe of her other shoe into the dirt. Julie would arrive soon. Julie, with her perfect blonde hair and snub nose. Her shoes that shone so bright they were blinding. Julie, with her trust fund that allowed her to get away with being the biggest B.I.T.C.H at school, and even though everyone knew it, they loved her anyway.

Ava would be happy to have a mum and dad who cared

enough to ask her how her day was, but that hadn't happened since she was five, so no point holding her breath there.

The snap of a twig startled Ava, and she turned her head just as Julie stepped up beside her.

"Lonely Ava, what happened to your friends? Did you send them away?" she sing-songed, her nose scrunched in a way that had Ava wishing the wind would change and forever leave Julie looking like she'd smelled horse poo.

Ava stood, ignoring the smirks covering Julie's friends' faces. They were clones of Julie, and, honestly, Ava couldn't tell them apart so she didn't bother to acknowledge them. Bracing herself, Ava scrunched her hands into tight fists, her nails biting into her soft flesh.

"I don't have it." Ava squared her shoulders, holding Julie's gaze.

Julie's eyes narrowed, her demeanour turning to a shade of black and ugly that matched the toe of Ava's shoes. *She was so toast.*

"That's a shame," Julie spat, her eyes gleaming in a way that belied her words. "We had a deal and you've broken it. You know you're gunna get it now, right?"

Ava's tummy rolled over, queasiness setting in before the punch to the gut had her doubling over. Pain ricocheted in every direction, her mouth filling with saliva that held a metallic hint. She spat on the ground, the slight tinge of red reflected against the concrete. She'd bitten her tongue.

Coughing, and ignoring the intense ache that refused to dissipate, she straightened again, waiting for the next blow.

"Hey!" Connor's voice sounded from somewhere over Ava's shoulder. She scrunched her nose and blinked, a new level of humiliation threatening.

Julie's face morphed from evil girl out to maim to a simpering doe-eyed flutter, her eyes focussed on the school's golden boy.

"Hey," Connor repeated, much closer now.

Connor Linton. High school's golden boy; owner of super-smart brain, golden-haired, beach-blue eyes, perfect looks and best mate of her older brother. *Somebody kill her.*

"Connor, hi!" Julie's perky voice set her teeth on edge.

Connor arrived at her side. She shuffled over and slumped back onto the bench she'd been waiting on. The pain she'd been holding at bay renewed itself with new vigour now that her shock had worn off. She hoped Connor wouldn't notice the tears threatening in the corners of her eyes. That really would be enough to ruin her school year.

Not because she had a thing for him. Not even *she* was that stupid. But because she *really* didn't want him blabbing her issues with Julie to her brother. The less Wyatt knew, the better. It was hard enough to maintain any sort of friendship with a brother she barely knew and could never visit.

"Hey." Connor nodded to Julie then turned to Ava. "Ava, you okay?"

"Yep. Just peachy," she muttered, hoping he didn't notice the croak in her voice.

Connor's ignorance of Julie didn't appear to stunt the other girl's attempt to capture his full attention.

"Connor, I caught your rugby game over the weekend. That goal you scored was just amazing."

He rolled his eyes, his expression had Ava lifting her lips just a little. At least Connor didn't appear to be falling at Julie's feet like most of the other boys at the private high school. It made her like him just a teensy bit more.

"Thanks, Julie. What I'd love to know, though, is why you punched Ava just now."

Ava froze. *Oh shoot. Connor saw that?* That was really not ideal. Unable to stop herself, her gaze swung to Julie, who gaped like a guppy fish at Connor. Her cheeks turned a shade of red that threatened to outshine the pristine ruby of her polo top.

Julie scrunched her nose and shrugged simultaneously. It wasn't her best look. "Ava started it. She owes me money she promised to give me back today, but when we came to meet her, she kicked dirt all over my shoes and told me I was a slut."

Ava gasped. "What? That's such a load of cra—"

Connor placed a hand on her shoulder, the move silencing her. She couldn't be sure if it was from pure shock at his touch, or the derisive look steeling his features. Had Connor Linton ever looked mad in her presence before? *Not that comes to mind. Mind you, I don't spend a lot of time within any vicinity of him either.*

"How much?" Connor asked, directing his words at Julie, his tone dangerously short.

Julie swallowed. "Fifty."

Without a word, Connor pulled his wallet from the back pocket of his jeans and fished out a few notes. Ava bent her head to the side to see better and could just make out a couple of twenties and fives.

He held the notes out to Julie, who hesitated for a second then snatched the money from him. She darted a quick look of hatred in Ava's direction, then with a huff, she stalked off. Her cronies followed behind, whispering with impressive speed but not loudly enough for Ava to decipher.

Frustration welled within Ava. "Why the hell did you do that?"

Connor diverted his gaze from Julie and her gang, then locked eyes with Ava, his brows raised. "Um…to stop them hurting you?" He shook his head, blue eyes wide with disbelief. "I couldn't very well ignore the fact Julie Barton was beating you up."

"Excuse me, but I wasn't being beaten up! It was a slight disagreement. I had it handled."

"Didn't look very handled to me, Ava."

"Look, just because you are besties with my brother doesn't mean I need your help or your charity. I'll pay you back."

"You don't nee—"

Ava clenched her teeth. "I said I'll pay you back, okay?"

Connor held his hands up, a grin threatening to break forth. "No need to get your knickers in a twist. I see you and your brother share that stubborn streak."

Ava bit her tongue. She couldn't be sure what her brother and her shared in terms of personality; they'd not grown up together. Their parents had split when Ava was just five, and her father had taken Wyatt. From what she could gather, they lived a happy and privileged existence. Ava was in the custody of their mum, who had never taken the split well. Of course, things had been bearable until a few years ago when her father had started dating again.

That was when life had really taken a nosedive.

"Earth to Ava?" Connor waved a hand in front of her face. "What?"

"I just asked if you needed a lift home? My dad's waiting, I'm sure he can give you a lift."

"No." As an afterthought, she tacked on, "Thanks though."

Connor pursed his lips, then did a half shrug. He turned and started walking away.

"Hey, Connor, just a second?" Ava closed the gap, trying to set aside the pain that movement brought to her core. She was pretty sure she'd have a bruise the size of Sydney Harbour by tomorrow.

"Changed your mind?"

"No, I don't need a lift. But I have a favour to ask."

"Yeah?"

"You can't tell Wyatt about this," Ava grabbed his arm, willing Connor to understand and not ask questions.

Connor rubbed at his ear. "Look, I don't know. Wyatt will be pissed if he finds out and I didn't tell him."

"Please. I know you're mates, but I just need your word you'll keep quiet." Connor dragged in a deep breath, a slight frown puckering his brows. She squeezed his arm gently before dropping her hand. "I'll tell him when I next see him." She crossed her fingers behind her back, having no intention to tell Wyatt anything.

"Fine." Connor narrowed his eyes at her, as though he could see right into her thoughts and knew her words were bogus. "But in return, you have to promise me something."

Ava swallowed. "Um…okay?"

"Promise me if Julie and her cohorts are tormenting you again, you come to me. They run around like they own the school, and it's not okay. You shouldn't let them push you around like that."

"Well, aren't you a regular superhero?" Ava grinned, enjoying being on the receiving end of his eye roll this time.

"Promise?" he persisted.

"It's a deal." She held her hand out, which he took, shaking it with a firm grasp. Ava let her hand fall limply to her side, tiny pinpricks dancing along her fingers. She gave a full-body shrug, then turned and walked in the opposite direction.

Current day

Ava was going to mess up.

Dammit! Why was everyone walking so slowly? She couldn't be late for this meeting. Gray Designs wasn't just any other architecture firm. It was *the* one. If she could make this project work, then maybe they'd offer her a position with the company. Not that she didn't love working as a contractor for Nexbo, but it would be nice to switch to a team who were more on the design side, not the development side.

Dodging another slow walker on Sydney's busy streets, she careened around a corner and smacked straight into a pole.

"Ahhh!"

Her knees crumpled beneath her, and she fell to the ground like a sack of cement. She'd never really understood the expression of 'seeing stars' before this moment, but right now she was seeing shooting stars and little singing Tweety birds. The type with high-pitched voices, for good measure.

She lay there in shock, her mind disconnected from her body. A haze of noise surrounded her, one persistent voice asking if she was okay.

Of course I'm not bloody okay. What if she'd dirtied her dress or grazed her knee? This wasn't the first impression she wanted to make. Gray Designs had been shopping around for a sustainability consultant for a few months now. Not that she'd had the courage to apply for the role, particularly since they weren't officially advertising it, but she would jump at the chance. She needed to make a good impression! There was the minor matter of her brother working there, but if she could prove herself through this project, then she could show them she was a perfect fit. Gray Designs had always been on Ava's list, but she'd never dreamed she'd have a shot at actually getting a job there.

They employed the cream-of-the-crop graduates. Not those who had only just cobbled through a second-rate university whilst supporting themselves by working three jobs.

"Can you hear me?" The voice persisted, and through her haze she focused on the man before her. Or standing above her, since she appeared to be lying flat on the ground. She cringed, the ache in her head increasing as her forehead puckered. *Yuck.* Sydney's sidewalk was not where she wanted to be lying right now. The dress she'd chosen for this meeting was crepe, thankfully a navy so deep it was almost black, but she'd die if it had pigeon poop ingrained down the back of it.

"Yes," she croaked, her throat raw. She couldn't be sure if that was because of a lack of air or panic at how her body didn't appear to be reacting as quickly as her mind. She did not have time for stupidly placed poles on city streets. Maybe she needed to write to city council and request they conduct a review.

"Let me help you inside. We can grab you a bottle of water or call a doctor? Are you able to sit up?"

The man's voice was kind, and her fuzziness was wearing off. At her nod, he assisted her to a seated position. A man with silver hair, partially covering his head, searched her eyes, concern crinkling the edges of his eyebrows. His wrinkled hand patted hers, a smile slipping easily into place, suggesting he was probably fairly happy with his life. Actually, the more she studied him, the more familiar he appeared.

"Wait—" she coughed and choked simultaneously "—you're Brian Gray." Now she knew why her throat was dry. "You started Gray Designs." *Way to go with stating the obvious, Ava.*

The man chuckled. "Yes, I am he. Are you able to tell me your name?"

"Ava. Ava De Vere," she added.

The older man's brows rose for a moment, but he didn't comment.

She gathered he'd made the connection between her and her brother. The one thing they'd always shared—their last name—though they'd not shared much else.

They certainly hadn't shared the same idyllic upbringing.

It was the only downside about taking this job at Gray Designs. The fact she might run into Wyatt. The thought sent her stomach into a tornado alongside her scrambled mind.

I'll just have to make sure I don't. It's a big company. Besides, he hates me; he's not likely to seek out a contractor.

At least, that was what she was banking on until she found her feet and could explain about the past. About her unforgivable actions. The letter she'd found of her mum's would be a great place to start. Her insides twisted at that thought.

"Well, Ava. It's lovely to meet you. Let me help you inside. Take my arm in case you're still a little groggy. That was quite the hit you took just now."

"Thank you. Yes, the post came from nowhere." Ava cringed immediately as she said the words; speaking without thought had never benefited her.

Brian chuckled. "Yes. One must watch those posts. They move around to blindside us when we least expect it."

Ava couldn't be sure if he was trying to be funny or laughing at her expense. His eyes appeared kind, though, so she assumed the former. She hobbled alongside him until they entered the double glass doors at the front of the building. A new building, designed by the firm's joint CEOs. Brian had hand-selected Lucas Knight years ago, grooming him to take over Gray Designs. Lucas had also fallen head-over-heels in love with Miranda, Brian's daughter. The two were now married.

Ava sighed. Oh, to be part of a family such as theirs. Hell, any family. She'd read a four-page spread in the latest *Women's Weekly* about Miranda Knight, née Gray. How having found love had changed her life and opened up her world. The article had pictured the pair bouncing a cute little girl on Lucas's knee, Miranda's protruding belly had been nestled against the girl's side. Brian Gray had featured in a few of the family pictures too.

They were the ultimate image of family happiness—not something Ava was familiar with.

"Ava, let's sit you here. I'll just ask Eloise on reception if she can grab you some water."

"Thank you." Ava glanced at her watch, she was late. *Three minutes and counting. Crap.*

She sucked in a deep breath and brushed away some dirt

smudges against the skirt of her fitted navy dress. Her palms ached, and when she flipped them over she saw red, raw skin, with pieces stripped away. Nothing to do about that. At least it wasn't actually bleeding. She'd grin and bear it. Right now she needed to get up to the top floor and her meeting with Miranda Knight. She could only hope the other woman would understand her delay. *Talk about unprofessional.*

Brian appeared at her side and sat on the plush lounge beside her, proffering a bottle of water.

"Thank you." The icy plastic was a relief against her palm as she took it. "I really appreciate your kindness, but I'm afraid I need to go. I know it seems rude, as you're helping me, but I'm late for a meeting with your daughter."

"Let's call her then. You should sit for a while. You really took a nasty knock to the head. I can see a nice red shiner building its way on your forehead. Eloise is going to bring down an ice-pack from the kitchen."

Ava twisted the lid and took a few gulps of water, buying some time to pull herself together. Tears were smarting in the corner of her eyes at the simple kindness. Goodness, she was such a wreck. Seeking comfort, she reached up and tugged at her earrings. She'd worn her favourite dangle four-leaf clover earrings—for luck.

"Thank you."

"Now, now. No need to tear up, or say thank you again. Three is plenty enough for a simple act of kindness. Why don't you tell me what you think of the building?"

Ava pursed her lips, the change in topic swift. The soft twinkle in Brian's eye suggested he was changing it on purpose, distracting her. How many ways could she be thankful right now? Instead of allowing the words to tip off her tongue—again—she took her time to survey the space. From where she sat in the lobby she couldn't take in the entire spectacular design, but she was very familiar with it.

Just another article topic she'd pored over in the past few years.

Designed by Lucas and Miranda, it wasn't the tallest of the new skyscrapers to grace the Darling Harbour end of George Street—the heart of Sydney City, if you asked her—but it was certainly the most eye-catching. Made almost entirely of recycled glass, its outer walls were angled in various ways to create a pattern that reflected light inside and out, depending on the time of day. To minimise environmental impact, the roof was composed of solar panels. There was also a rooftop garden designed by a landscape architect who'd done such a fabulous job they'd offered him a permanent position.

That was what Ava wanted. Desperately.

The interior where she currently sat also showed a wall of glass, much like being in a fishbowl, except every second panel was etched glass, giving the viewer a sense of fascination instead of being under the microscope. It was clever. Everything about the building was clever. She'd always thought so from the first moment they had built it.

"It's amazing," she said at last. Understatement of the year, and she admonished herself for her lack of descriptive skills. Every time she opened her mouth, she encountered another verbal disaster. "I particularly love how sustainable Lucas and Miranda made it. The recycled materials used show they have thought it through from a climate-change perspective. It's about bringing architecture into the current times, which is something I'm really passionate about."

She opened her mouth to add something else but stopped short when a group of three emerged from the lift just to the left of the reception desk.

Lucas Knight, Miranda Knight and, *oh,* could the world kill her and swallow her whole.

It couldn't be.

Why did *he* have to work here too?

Connor Linton.

Best friend to her brother and a blast from her past she wasn't really interested in facing. Now or ever again.

She cleared her throat, which had gone tighter than the nut between a cement bolt. Brian threw her a reassuring smile, which tilted into a curious frown. *Perfect.* Ava did her best to arrange her features into a neutral position.

Easier said than done.

Miranda said something that elicited a chuckle from the other two men. They were all still too far away for her to hear their exact words. A pang resounded in the pit of Ava's stomach.

Working here would be an absolute dream come true, but how would that work if she had to run into Connor Linton? And her brother? She swallowed. *One step at a time.* She'd just have to find a way to make peace with her past. A chance at working here was worth that uncomfortable conversation, wasn't it?

Connor hadn't appeared to change a lot since she'd last seen him. Sure, he was older and, okay, perhaps a tad better looking. How was that fair? He wore a suit like a second skin; the material stretched taut across broad shoulders and hard thighs, his legs longer than Bondi Beach. Both men were tall, akin to a pair of skyscrapers as they strode towards her. She rolled her eyes at her own visual. Lucas wore black and had a slimmer build, whereas Connor wore blue and was like the burlier brighter version. The vibrant colour suited him, particularly when set off by his stark white shirt—no tie.

Ava swept a quick look at Brian, and then at Lucas. Both of them wore ties. Hope flared. Maybe Connor was just here for a chat. Perhaps he didn't even work here. Her chest eased a little. Except why was he here? The constriction came back full force. Was he interviewing for a job? The only role she knew Gray Designs to be actively looking for was the one she coveted.

Wouldn't she know if Connor Linton had gone into sustainability consultation? It was a minor industry. Ava was one of the best and made it her job to know everyone else in the field.

Her gaze returned to Connor.

Busted.

Clear blue eyes zeroed in on her, their widths expanding a little before a smile slid across his face in greeting. That trademark little quirk at the corner of his mouth. Gah. Why did she have to remember that about him? Of all things? A tingle shimmied in her tummy, and she squirmed. Uncrossing her legs, she crossed them the other way, trying to ward off the unwanted jitters.

She still did not know why Connor was here.

The trio reached her and Brian's side.

"Hey, Dad," Miranda said, leaning down to place a kiss against Brian's cheek before she straightened and focused her attention on Ava. "And you must be Ava, my eleven o'clock. How are you feeling? I heard you had an incident with an errant street pole?"

Tell-tale heat suffused Ava's cheeks. What she wouldn't do for a block of cheese right about now. Some spicy cheddar to bring down her anxiety levels, which had just skyrocketed at the attention she was receiving on all fronts. A quick glance at Connor showed he was sporting an amused expression. Not daring to look at anyone else, she focused on Miranda. The other woman wore a fitted dress, her baby bump poking out of the sleek jacket she wore over the top. Her stance was so casual, so at home with her position at the helm of the company. Ava equally envied and congratulated her on that self-confidence. She appeared genuinely concerned, no hint of humour at the situation, unlike what she seemed to be getting from someone else.

"Yep," she choked and tried again. "Yes. I'm Ava De Vere." She stood, proffering her hand.

Her vision blurred for a second and a warm hand grabbed her arm, guiding her back to a seated position. "Steady on, love. You really rammed into that pole."

She blinked, attempting to clear the murky grey and sprinkles that were dancing at her periphery. This was *so* not how she'd wanted today to go.

Miranda sat to Ava's left, her hand resting on Ava's shoulder. The care and attention she was receiving from two almost strangers was going to make Ava tear up again. "Let's just sit here and have a chat. Are you sure you don't want us to call a doctor?"

"Or your brother?" Connor stated, like a stab to her already crumbling composure.

Oh sure, let's call Wyatt and completely shred away the last of her dignity. He'd probably just laugh at her stupidity, then yell at her again.

Ava lifted her head, glaring at Connor, willing him to shut the hell up.

The fool had the nerve to smirk, holding his hands up with a chuckle. "Hey, just trying to help."

Brian looked from Connor to Ava and back again. "Do you two know each other?"

Ava rolled a few responses around in her head, assessing and discarding them as quickly as she could.

Connor must have decided she would not respond. "Ava and I went to high-school together. Briefly. She's Wyatt's younger sister."

As if that explained it all.

"Our in house counsel, Wyatt?" Miranda queried.

"The one and only," Connor quipped, a grin still shadowing the corners of his mouth.

Our? Guess that confirms Connor does work here.

Ava threw Connor another glare for good measure. "Yes. Wyatt is my brother," she snapped. "We haven't spoken in nearly twelve years, though. I doubt he's going to want to hear from me."

And why the hell had she told them all that?

Connor rubbed at the back of his ear, the grin falling from his face, a sure sign her words had made everyone awkward.

Wonderful. Just. Bloody. Wonderful.

Years on, even so, her family dynamic was helping her ruin her life. Would she ever learn?

* * *

Connor took in the pale yet determined face of his best friend's younger sister. Ava had always been a spitfire by nature—fight back when under attack, or under any sort of duress, really.

Years didn't appear to have numbed that tendency to fight first, even if it had changed her in other ways. Her appearance for one. He'd have struggled to correlate the auburn-haired beauty sitting before him with the mousey and belligerent teen he'd known. Except for her eyes, they didn't appear to have changed one iota.

He wanted to kick himself for mentioning Wyatt's name, but Ava was sporting a solid bump on her forehead and, honestly, he'd thought maybe she needed someone familiar. Family was always who he thought of first when times got tough. Not that Wyatt ever mentioned Ava. In fact, last he'd heard, she was *persona non grata* to him, but it was the only connection he knew for her.

Dumbass move. Clearly. If looks could kill he'd be a shrivelled molten mess right now.

He cleared his throat. "Lucas, we'd better go, mate, or we'll miss the meeting."

Lucas, his boss and his mentor, nodded, a look of concern still gracing his features. Miranda gave her husband a curt nod, which he reciprocated, Brian offering one too.

Was Ava here for a job interview?

He didn't know what openings were going at the moment, but that wasn't anything new. His head only had enough space for his current project. Just thinking of the new convention centre design gave him a lift. This was finally his chance to do justice to his father's memory. So long as Ava's job wasn't anything to do with him, he was happy for her. He had enough family drama on his plate without inviting himself into more through his best friend.

"Are you meeting at the site or Nexbo head office?" Miranda asked, her gaze on Lucas before flicking to encompass Connor.

"The site. We're going to walk," Lucas replied.

"We need to iron out a few ideas," Connor added. "Apparently my design is spectacular but possibly not hitting the regulations on all fronts." He couldn't help but smirk. Lucas was solidly behind him on his ideas, but Nexbo had hinted local government was pushing back. Apparently the new convention centre had to be award-winning, but also sustainably focused. Nexbo, the developers, thought the hoops they had to jump through were a croc of shit, but hey, so long as they signed off his design, that was their problem. Wyatt had already put in a billion hours to help pave the way with the government, so surely they'd now be fine.

Designing the new convention centre that would grace the shores of Sydney Harbour was going to put Connor Linton's name right where he'd always wanted it: Award-winning. Talented. The best. And he'd make sure his father's name was right up there alongside his.

Just like they'd always planned.

He nodded to Brian, Ava and Miranda, ignoring the pang of emptiness that now burrowed into his gut. "We'll see you later."

Both Brian and Miranda offered him a smile. Ava seemed to have gone into her shell, keeping her gaze on her fingers clasped tightly in her lap. Her knuckles were a shade or three whiter than normal. He glimpsed a fine gold band on her middle finger, the same finger she'd thrown at him the last time they'd spoken.

Typical Ava behaviour.

Connor followed Lucas out of the building, pocketing his hands as he allowed his thoughts to drift. He and Ava may not have ever been that close, but Connor had always felt bad for her. He'd sworn an oath of secrecy, and other than one tiny slip up, he hadn't ever told anyone just how hard Ava's life at school had been. If his sisters had been copping the sort of shit she had from the resident mean girls, he'd have done anything to ensure it stopped.

Could he have done more for her back then? *Probably.*

Did she let him? *Hell no.*

And now it was none of his sweet business. Just the way he liked it.

"You're quiet." Lucas stepped around a group of tourists who were blocking half the path.

Connor would never understand why people in groups thought standing three abreast on a tiny walkway was a solid idea. But then, people could be certifiably stupid about a lot of things.

"Just pondering ideas. Do you think Nexbo are going to say yes to our latest proposal?"

"Possibly. I think the government are going to cause some

issues though." Lucas paused, throwing Connor a quick look that instantly put him on high alert. "So you know Ava."

A leading statement if ever Connor had heard one.

"Yes. I think we've established that." He stretched, shrugging a shoulder, easing some tension that was growing there.

"You didn't say hello to her or ask if she's okay. I thought you and Wyatt were close?"

"We are. But you heard Ava, she and her brother don't talk. Wyatt hasn't seen her in years. I'm not one to get involved in other people's drama."

He heard the frustration in his voice and puffed out a breath. He wasn't sure where Lucas was going with this.

"But you and she get along okay?" Lucas persisted.

Sure. They got along. About as well as anyone could with a prickly-as-hell echidna. Though he had to admit, she had grown into her looks a little more than he'd remembered. Dammit, why did his head go there again?

"I haven't seen her in over twelve years, but we used to be friends." He paused on the last word, rubbing at the side of his chin. "Of a sort."

"Do you think you'd be able to work with her?"

Connor stalled. Lucas took a few steps before he must have realised Connor had stopped walking. "Why would I need to work with Ava?" Connor asked, suspicion and dread crowding every word.

Lucas took a few steps back and slapped a hand on Connor's chest. "Because Nexbo are insisting we hire a sustainability consultant for this project. And you just met her."

Oh, shit-a-brick.

2

Connor slung a towel around his neck, panting. His workout had helped. At least a little. Punching the crap out of a punching bag and pounding the dilapidated treadmill usually did.

Today it hadn't fully exorcised the frustration that flowed through him. His project, his baby, was being derailed.

Not only were Gray Designs being forced to bring on Nexbo's sustainability consultant, but they were also bringing on Ava De Vere, and she was going to be looking over his shoulder until this project finished.

Talk about a complication he could live without right now.

Wyatt was going to lose his mind.

He flopped onto one of the plastic chairs at the outer edge of the gym. It wasn't much of a gym—more a warehouse that held a few bits of equipment and a big arse sound system that was always blasting hip hop music. He wasn't a fan of their music tastes, but the place was cheap and there weren't any hotties running around in Spandex looking for a date.

Hell, when was the last time he'd even been on a date? He dropped his head to his hands, swiping at the sweat caking his forehead. It had been a while. Who had the time? Between work and checking in on his mum and sisters, there weren't a lot of hours left in the day.

He should see if some guys from the office wanted to go play a game of rugby on the weekend, maybe grab a beer or two afterwards. They could go to Coogee. The girls there were always pretty fine to look at. Perhaps a casual hook-up was just what he needed to get some stress out of his system.

He cringed at his own thoughts, his stomach knotting at the thought of how callous they sounded.

A body slumped onto the chair next to him, half nudging him out of his own seat. "You're not gonna get any fitter by crying into your palms."

Connor looked to his left, then narrowed his eyes at his friend. "Stuff you, Wyatt. I've been here for an hour. What happened to you?" He sat up, a shit-eating grin slipping into place. "You getting your arse handed to you by your girl-friend again?"

"Least I'm getting some action," Wyatt threw back. "I saw you at the bags and decided I'd leave you to whatever tantrum you were working through. I've been out collecting kilometres on the pavement. Need to rack up the time now since I don't think I'll get much next week." He waggled his eyebrows, and Connor sent him a derogatory eye roll.

"When do you and Evette leave? Where are you going again?"

"Whitsundays. Sunday morning. One week of pure bliss. Actually, speaking of my girlfriend, I'm thinking, uh—" he cleared his throat, suddenly looking nervous "—I thought it might be time to, you know, tie the knot."

Connor choked on air. "You're kidding."

Wyatt folded his bottom lip under, nodding his head, as though he were pondering Connor's reaction and breaking it down. "Actually, no. I'm serious. I'm not getting any younger."

Connor snorted, still not buying if Wyatt was serious. Wyatt and Evette had been dating for over a year now, but Connor would be hard-pressed to say she was a perfect fit for his mate. She was nice enough, and easy on the eyes, but there was a mean streak to her personality that popped out occasionally. Not that he'd be sharing those views.

"Yeah, we're ancient. Thirty-two and on a downhill slide. I have noticed your hairline's getting a bit peppered with grey. I'll buy you some hair dye."

"You still think I'm joking."

Connor took stock of his friend. Brown eyes stared back. Serious.

Shit.

"Right." Connor's stomach roiled, and he had to bite back the urge to tell his friend he was making a diabolical mistake. "Yeah, well… Evette's a pretty nice girl. Have you bought a ring?"

Wyatt burst out laughing. "You should see your face. It's like a cat's bum."

Connor slapped Wyatt on the back, hard enough to push the other guy half out of his seat, and then stood. Neither of them were short, both having reached six-foot in their early teens, but where Wyatt had a slimmer build, Connor was all muscle. Years of rugby had honed his torso, and he made it a point of pride not to lose that shape. Even if most of his time was now spent behind a computer looking at cads and at his drawing board.

His dad had always said for every hour he spent at the computer designing, he needed to spend at least ten minutes pumping iron. His dad who had been his fiercest supporter and confidant. Until a cruel twist of science had stolen him from Connor's life. Far too soon. Leaving Connor with a mum who couldn't function and two much younger sisters who'd struggled to cope.

Life could suck sometimes, which is why Connor was all about living in the moment and not weighing his life down with any more responsibilities or complications. He'd yet to break the news to Wyatt about the biggest complication to enter his life.

"So you're not serious about getting hitched? Or you are? I'll be honest, man, right now I actually can't tell."

Wyatt dragged himself to a standing position and shrugged. "I love her, so yeah. I'm serious."

Connor didn't like the taste that statement left in his mouth. Evette could be whiney when not getting her own way, and something about her pricked at his conscious.

"Good luck." Connor stated. He tugged on either ends of the towel draped around his neck. "I have something else we need to talk about though."

Wyatt headed towards the showers. "Shoot. I gotta freshen up. Evette's coming over tonight."

"Wait." Connor jogged to catch up with his friend. "You're not going to ask her tonight are you?"

Wyatt cocked a brow and shook his head a little. "I have style, unlike you. Of course, I'm not going to just pitch the idea on her. These matters take planning and finesse. You should look those up."

Connor threw a lazy punch at his mate's arm. "I'll leave that to you, and whilst you're at the thesaurus, look up deodorant. You smell like my gym bag."

They reached the bathroom block. Like the rest of the gym, it wasn't state of the art, but it had three showers that were kept clean through a weekly dousing of bleach. Connor knew never to come on Tuesdays for that very reason. One wall housed a row of lockers big enough to hang a suit if he needed to fit in an early workout. Just as he reached the locker to the far left, which he'd nabbed for the evening, his mobile rang.

"What was it you wanted to talk about?" Wyatt interrupted, banging open the locker door three down from where Connor stood.

"Just a tick," Connor said, yanking on the rusty padlock that was refusing to budge. *I really need to replace this sucker.* He yanked once more, and the lock gave way just as his phone stopped. "Sorry, this might be Lucas." He pulled his phone from the side pocket of his laptop backpack and swiped at the screen, expecting to see Lucas's name.

It was an unknown number. Connor stared at the screen for a beat longer, tossing up whether to call back. A beep indicated they'd left a voicemail.

"Was it Lucas?" Wyatt asked, already stripping off his shirt.

"Nah," Connor murmured, and went to put the phone back when it beeped again, this time showing an incoming text message from the same unknown number. He clicked on it and briefly read the message, his stomach tying into tighter knots with each word. Not even a full day in and Ava was putting him in the middle.

"Earth to Connor? If it's not Lucas, who is it? It's not your mum, is it?"

Connor darted a look at his friend. Wyatt was the only person in the world he'd ever told about the situation with his mum. "No, not Mum. I have to take it though. Let's grab a beer tomorrow afternoon?"

"You're being pretty cagey, dude. You met someone or something?"

Panic tore through Connor's chest. "Hell no! It's not that sort of call."

Ava was the last person in the world who he'd want to get involved with.

Wyatt raised both brows, a smirk hovering at his lips. "That was an adamant denial, but whatever, man. Text me a time tomorrow." He shoved his gym gear into the locker and grabbed his towel, wrapping it loosely around his hips before heading into one of the shower stalls.

Connor smacked his phone against his palm a few times before he shoved it into the pocket of his shorts. He grabbed his backpack and slung it over his shoulder. He waited until he was two blocks away from the gym before he fished his phone back out and hit redial.

"Hello, Connor?" Her voice was soft, husky and feminine. The fact he noticed irritated the crap out of him.

"What's going on, Ava?" he snapped. "Why can't I tell your brother you got the job?"

She sighed. "Can we meet for a drink somewhere? It will take a while to explain."

"Fine. But you're buying." Connor named a place to meet in about twenty minutes, then hung up.

This should be fun.

* * *

Ava fiddled with the stem of her glass of rosé. The pub Connor had named was in Surry Hills, just around the corner from where Ava lived. Or rented… for now. A glow of warmth spread through her at the thought she'd be working at Gray Designs, even in a consultancy capacity.

If she impressed on this contract, she might land a full-time position, and then her days of living in the rental wave could be relegated to the past. She'd be part of a family. She could put down roots and really make herself a home.

She took a deep swig of her wine, enjoying the fruity aftertaste. She needed this job to work out, which is why she didn't want Connor ratting her out to Wyatt just yet.

Wyatt would find out eventually. She wasn't fool enough to think she could fly under the radar at Gray Designs indefinitely. But she'd prefer to be the one to break the news to him once she worked out how on Earth she could talk to him again. To mend the bond she'd well and truly broken.

Thanks a lot for that one, Mum. Again.

She brushed at a fly circling the rim of her glass. If only swatting away memories of that evening were as easy as shooing a fly. She'd not spoken to her mother since and did her best not to think of the woman.

Tipping the glass back, she finished the last drops, then turned her left wrist and checked the time. Five more minutes until Connor said he'd be there. She probably shouldn't order another drink, but she was celebrating. It might be a solo celebration, and one she planned to take home after her chat with Connor to complete with a block of cheese and the latest regency romance she'd downloaded to her kindle.

Just as she was about to move, a hand plonked a glass onto the table before her. She followed the muscled forearm and looked up, and up. Sweat glued his gym shirt to his broad chest. She read the single word blazoned across his pecs. Freedom. Intriguing choice. Her eyes lifted to his corded neck, a pulse beating at the base of his collarbone. His chiselled jawline was covered in day old scruff. And his mouth that twisted, lips pressed together.

Connor.

"Hi," Ava croaked.

"You finished?"

"Sorry." Ava had the good graces to blush. She snatched at the glass and took a hefty swig. There was no way she thought of Connor like that. She'd just been... distracted. Had she noticed before how nice his arms were?

Don't go there, Ava.

"Thank you for the drink," she tacked on belatedly.

Connor sat on the stool next to her, offering a nod at her words. He took a long swallow of beer before he placed it down before him. His hand stayed on the glass, gripping it tight. He cleared his throat. "So…"

"Soo…?" Ava repeated.

"You needed to talk?"

"Oh, yes." Jeez, what was wrong with her? Her mind had turned to soggy noodles. "I don't want you to tell Wyatt about me getting the job."

"Yes, I got that bit. You're certifiable if you think I'm going to lie to him. He's our in-house counsel. He's going to find out." Connor spun his glass in a half twist and then started drawing lines in the condensation.

"The drinks were supposed to be my shout," Ava replied, changing the subject.

Connor took a slow sip, assessing her over the rim of his glass. "Are you stalling?"

"Maybe a little." She flicked a nervous smile his way.

"Fine. You can buy the next round. I assume you're celebrating? I wasn't aware you'd gone into the building business."

Ava swallowed, feeling the tightness in her chest loosen a little. "Yes. I'm still a little blown away that I'll get to work with Gray Designs on such a major project. Not that I'm not good. I mean I am good. Just that after the head knock and subsequent decimated meeting, it was a surprise they were still happy for me to do the job."

"Miranda and Lucas run a tight ship. If they hired you, it's because you're the best."

Warmth spread through Ava's chest at the unexpected respect in Connor's voice.

"Well, I guess it was Nexbo who hired me, but they said it

was Gray's ultimate choice. I'll work really hard. You won't need to worry."

"I'm not," Connor quipped. His eyes flashed to hers then darted away. "We might need to lay some ground rules though, because I've waited a really long time for a chance like this to come up, and I'm not planning to budge much from my current design. Or at all."

A hint of steel threaded those words, and Ava felt her first hiccup over the role. She'd been so focused on the opportunity, and then worrying over how she'd keep the news from her brother for as long as she could, that she hadn't fully explored the fact that she'd be working closely with Connor. His was the project she'd be consulting on. Making this work would be the difference between her potentially getting more work with Gray Designs, so she needed to shine.

She needed to work *with* Connor.

He levelled his gaze against hers, and she leaned in a little, offering a brief nod. A heady mix of masculine sweat, musk, cinnamon and something else she couldn't define hit her nose, coating her senses with the appealing smell. She shifted, suddenly aware of how close she and Connor were sitting to one another.

Her thigh brushed against his, the heat and hard length sent tingles shooting down her sides. Her fitted dress felt a little tighter than normal around her chest.

Her heart skittered, an awareness flowing throughout her entire body that could mean only one thing.

Attraction.

But, no, that was ludicrous.

Had she drunk too much?

Probably. Plus, it had been a while. And Connor *was* attractive. That wasn't disputable, and he was all sweaty and giving her his undivided attention. That was all. Circumstance.

Mentally willing her body to calm the hell down, she finished the last of the wine in her glass.

"Another?" she offered, noting he'd now finished his beer and was continuing to draw lines on the other side of this glass.

He rubbed at his jaw, then hid a yawn. "Yeah, sure, one more wouldn't hurt. I might need to grab a burger or something. I missed lunch. Should I grab us some menus? I don't know that you should drink too much more without some food either."

Indignation shot through Ava. "I'm not drunk."

Connor held his palms up. "I didn't say you were. Only that this would be your third glass of wine, that I know of, and you're pretty slim." His eyes darted from her face to her chest and downwards before flying back up to her face again. His eyes widened a little, and he made an odd type of choke. He pushed himself up and muttered about going to find menus before he walked off.

Ava tracked his movements. Workout gear really suited Connor, and she'd be lying if she didn't notice how nice his butt looked in those shorts. He ambled, a bit like a giant bear, his broad shoulders certainly filling out the full expanse of his T-shirt.

She wasn't the only one who noticed. A group of women wearing work dresses similar in style to hers tracked Connor's movements as he passed their table. One woman whispered to her friend and slid off her stool, prancing inside through the glass sliding doors, presumably to follow Connor.

Ava turned back to her table. Nothing to do with her. Connor's dating life was definitely not something she wanted to know about.

3

Connor leaned his forearms against the bar, waiting for the waitress to finish pouring a couple of beers for a group of guys sitting on the other side of the bar from where he stood.

There weren't any physical menus that he could see at the bar, but he'd ask. Women could be picky with food. God, didn't he know that.

A warm hand landed on his shoulder. He flicked a glance to see if it belonged to Ava.

He should have known from the overpowering scent of roses that it wasn't. Ava's perfume had been subtle, a light floral that tingled his nose but didn't make him want to sneeze and rub his face like this one did.

"Hey." The blonde he'd noticed outside pouted back at him.

"Hey," he returned. She was hot, but right now he wasn't in the mood. He wanted food and a decent night's sleep. Collecting a woman on his way home did not fit into those plans. Besides, Ava was waiting outside for him, and she still hadn't fully explained why he couldn't spill her news to Wyatt. It was bugging him, her putting him in the middle. He also needed to check in on his mum before this never-ending day was over.

He frowned. Did Ava really think she'd get away with Wyatt not finding out for any length of time? Whatever the issue was between those two, he just wanted them to sort it out—without his input.

"Hellooo?" the blonde said, presumably again given her impatient tone.

"Sorry." Connor removed her hand from his arm and shrugged. "I'm here with someone."

The blonde pursed her lips to one side. "Can't blame a girl for trying. You're gorgeous." She offered a sultry smile then sauntered away, leaving Connor still waiting for the server.

How long does it take to order a beer?

Connor looked about, spotting an errant menu on a table not far from the bar. He snagged it and went straight to the burgers. Cheeseburger looked good. Pulling his phone out, he rang Ava who answered after one ring.

"Why are you calling me? Did you decide to do a runner?"

"No. But the bar staff are few and far between. I thought I'd order whilst I'm already here. What do you feel like?"

"Oh." She sounded surprised. "What are you getting?"

"Cheeseburger."

"Sounds good. I'll get the same."

Connor quirked a brow. "You don't want to know the options? Or give me a list of five things you'd like to change in the meal?"

Ava snort-laughed. "Nah, however it comes. I'd love to know why you assume women are picky eaters, though. Have all your girlfriends been like that?"

"Not exactly," he replied. "Are you happy with the same wine?"

"Yeah, sure. I'm *not* picky."

Connor smiled at that and hung up. She certainly wasn't.

If he'd brought his sisters here, he'd have to take notes for their orders.

The server finally decided it was his turn. After ordering, he shoved the table number and cutlery under his arm and carried their drinks out to where Ava sat. She'd chosen a wooden table situated off to one side in the beer garden. It was a fairly small area, with only a handful of tables scattered around the space. Cobbled pavement coated the ground, and fairy lights hung from post to post across the area. The balmy night air had set in with the farewell of the summer sun; perfect weather for sitting outside for a few drinks and burger on a Friday night.

Too bad his weekend didn't look as exciting. There was washing to sort, and cleaning of both his studio and his mum's house. If his sisters were around, he'd need to organise groceries with them and work out a schedule on who would ensure their mum ate properly. No way would he allow a repeat of last year on that front.

He needed to pin Clare, the older of his two younger sisters, down to ensure she was covering her rent with her part-time job. They'd argued about her getting the work. He didn't want her to blow her studies for the sake of earning money when he could afford to pay that for her.

"Here you go," Ava said as he sat. She held out a fifty-dollar note to him.

He waved her off. "It's fine. You can get the food next time."

She raised a brow but didn't argue with him, instead shoving the note into the side pocket of her dress. The move pulled the dress even tighter across her chest and Connor had to look away. Now was not the time to notice his best friend's little sister had become all woman. The last time he'd seen Ava, she'd given him the finger simply for offering her a lift to school.

She'd aged well in the interim years.

"What did you mean when you said not exactly?" Ava asked, breaking him from his musing.

He took a sip of his beer, trying to place when he'd said that but coming up blank. "Sorry?"

"Your predisposition to assume all females are picky eaters."

"Oh. Well… My sisters are, that's all."

"Are you and your sisters still really close? I know they were younger than you."

"Yes. We're close. They still live at home. After—" he swallowed "—after my dad passed, I took over the cooking. They were ten and eight, and it reached nightmarish levels. Let's just say I've always learned to offer a woman all the food options."

Ava's eyes widened, a soft sad look entering their depths. "Connor, I'm so sorry. I didn't know your dad passed away. If the girls were that young, it must have happened a while ago."

"Yeah. Just after high school."

Connor shifted uncomfortably. He didn't enjoy talking about that time of his life. He'd gone from top of the world with every opportunity open to him, to a pit of hell.

Ava reached out her hand and squeezed his. Her fingers were so small wrapped around his giant fist, her nails neatly cropped and bare of any nail polish.

"It's never easy to lose a parent."

"No, it's not." Connor couldn't remember the last time he'd had a woman hold his hand. It felt… nice. He shifted his palm, grabbing for his beer. "So. The time has come, Ava De Vere. You need to let me know why I can't tell Wyatt."

Ava dived for her wine glass again, taking a big gulp. He worried she was going to scull the whole thing for a moment; she appeared so desperate.

"I just need some time to tell him myself, that's all. I promise I will tell him, but it needs to come from me. He hates me, which I don't blame him for. I would like to mend fences with him. Over what happened at his dad's wedding."

Connor hadn't been able to make it to the wedding, but he'd heard the aftershocks when Wyatt turned up to his house afterwards, royally pissed at his sister. Instead of asking Wyatt for details, they'd just gotten drunk. Connor paused at Ava's use of the term *"his dad"*. "Isn't he your dad too?"

"Only by birth," Ava replied with a casual shrug. She appeared to be aiming for nonchalance, but Connor could see otherwise. She swallowed before her eyes darted away.

Connor had never really understood the dynamics of how that all worked. All he knew was that when Wyatt had been ten and Ava five, their parents had split. Instead of joint custody, they'd each taken a child. Wyatt hadn't ever spoken about his mum again after that time. He'd told Connor once that he'd tried to be friends with Ava, but she'd blocked him from her life. For a brief few years they'd all gone to the same Sydney private high school, but Wyatt and Ava had never been friends.

"Well, at least that's what I was always told," Ava continued. "That's part of the something I need to discuss with Wyatt."

Connor sucked in a deep breath. "That sounds complicated."

"It is. Does Wyatt ever say anything about me? Is he still mad about cars?"

"C'mon, Ava. Don't put me in the middle of this. Wyatt's my best mate. Whatever issues you two have are your own."

Ava nibbled at her thumb, staring into her glass. She looked lost. And quite small, as if his words had sucked some air from her lungs.

He opened his mouth to say something but shut it again as the server appeared and placed two giant plates down in front of them. The cheeseburger looked delicious, complete with a glossy bun and golden chips flecked with a spicy seasoning. Too bad his appetite had disappeared.

Something inside him twigged; maybe Ava wasn't exactly the person he'd always assumed her to be. He'd tried to help her when they were at school, but maybe he hadn't done enough? He had a bad feeling that not telling Wyatt he was about to be working closely with his sister was going to come back and bite him on the arse.

* * *

Ava's heels clipped the pavement, echoing through her quiet street as she turned into the front courtyard of her apartment building. A whisper of wind whipped her hair across her face, so she brushed it behind her ear and made her way up the steps to the door.

Ava had waved off Connor's offer to escort her home, though she had promised to send him a text the minute she stepped through the door. His insistence had left her with a funny wobble in her tummy, probably due to the simple fact no one had ever cared that much about her to make sure she'd make it home safely.

Connor had made her promise, as if it was just a matter of fact, like he'd ask any friend or colleague to do the same. Yet it changed something within Ava.

It meant so much more to her than it should, which could end up being dangerous if she let it.

There was no room in her plans to fall for Wyatt's best friend—she had only two things she wanted right now: deliver on the convention centre project to Nexbo and show Gray Designs she should be on their payroll full time. Bonus points if she sorted out her past with Wyatt, though she wasn't holding her breath there.

She pulled her key card from her purse and swiped it against the security door to the apartment building. After a short beep, she pushed the heavy door inwards, immediately bombarded with a rush of cool air.

Strata always seemed to set the air conditioning to freezing in the communal areas. It drove Ava nuts, given she had more of a penchant for fresh air. Not that she didn't appreciate it on the forty-degree days, but today hadn't been that and she liked the soupy warmth that still clung to the evening outside.

Summer in Sydney. Was anything more beautiful?

It had become her haven, her starting point to this fresh path in her life—a far cry from the one she'd grown up in.

Taking the stairs up to her apartment on the second floor, Ava inserted her key in the lock and opened the door, flicking lights on as she stepped into her sanctuary.

She barely remembered the time she'd been part of a family. All she could remember was her mother taking her away. At first it had been nice, her mum had doted on her and been her universe. Then it had changed. A day she could recall so clearly... Her mother, Vanessa, had collected her from school in a total rage.

Ava's father had met someone else.

Ava was eight at the time. She'd always wondered about her mysterious father. The man who gave them money, paying for what seemed to be quite a lavish lifestyle, but who she didn't know and who didn't want to know her. He'd been part of her creation, yet he'd walked away from her life, as though she'd never existed.

She'd never had the courage to ask that question, though it haunted her every waking moment and sometimes her dreams.

"No." Ava slammed the door behind her, clenched her fists, and lightly tapped her forehead to the wooden panel. She wouldn't allow her win today to be clouded by the memories of her past.

Giving herself a mental and physical shake, she went to the kitchen and pulled a block of Gouda cheese and a half empty bottle of wine from the fridge. After pouring herself a glass, she took it and the full block of cheese out to her tiny balcony. The view wasn't much, facing the inside courtyard of the apartment block, but it was spacious enough to hold a small coffee table and two chairs. Taking the chair to her right, Ava placed her glass down after a quick sip. She tore the paper from the block of cheese, biting a chunk off the end. She chewed, contemplating her day.

A quick beep sounded from inside.

"Dammit." *So much for sitting and relaxing.*

She walked backed inside to where she'd tossed her phone onto the kitchen bench, Connor's name flashed on the screen.

Connor: You haven't messaged.

She grinned.

Ava: Oops, sorry. I'm home. Thank you for dinner.

Little dots appeared on her screen before disappearing only to appear back a moment later.

. . .

Connor: You know it's not very nice to say you'll message and then not do so.

Ava frowned. Was he actually cross with her? She tapped out her reply, adding a winking emoji, then hit send.

Ava: Sorry, Dad.

Ava stared at her phone, taking it out to her balcony and her block of cheese, waiting for another response. After about five minutes, she gave up and turned her phone to silent. Connor was certainly a mystery that she had no intention of solving. She felt a little negligent, given he had been so insistent on her checking in. She'd planned to text him…

Enough.

Tomorrow was the weekend, and she had two complete days to bask in the glow of having gotten her foot in the door of Gray Designs.

She might not be ready to face Wyatt right now, but first steps and all that. If she was around for a longer term, maybe Wyatt would eventually forgive her. And then maybe she'd have a chance of explaining what the hell had been going on all those years ago.

* * *

Connor threw his backpack onto the couch as he entered his small studio. The lights were still on at the main house. He hesitated over going straight there. It was after nine, but he hoped his mum had actually eaten something. There was washing he wanted to make a start on, he could take that over now. His suits he'd deliver to the dry cleaners in the morning.

He grimaced at his own thoughts. How lame did that sound? Thirty-two-year-old bachelor who still lived at home, albeit in a studio he'd had built so he wasn't physically still in his childhood house, and his grand plans for the weekend revolved around laundry. And cleaning.

He needed to organise that game of rugby with the boys, purely so he had something on that wasn't totally domesticated.

After grabbing a few armfuls of washing that were tossed about his space, he made the short distance to the back door, walking through into the laundry.

"That you, Connor?" His mum's voice floated from the TV room, muted background voices suggested she was watching the television.

"Yeah, Mum, it's me. I'm just putting a load on. Have you got washing that needs doing?"

He picked up the box of powder and threw some over the clothes he'd already placed in the giant barrel. A few of his sisters' clothes were in the dirty clothes basket, so he collected those up and added them to his load.

"Hello, sweetheart," his mum said from the doorway. "You shouldn't be doing our washing on a Friday night. Surely there are plenty of women out there you could take to dinner or to a movie?"

Connor walked over and wrapped his mum in a hug. She seemed to have shrunk over the years, or maybe that was just an illusion. At least she had a little colour in her cheeks today. When he'd popped his head in to check on her before leaving for work this morning, she'd been very pale. He stepped away again, taking the few pieces of clothing she was clutching in her hands, and added them to the load. He flipped the lid down and pressed start.

"There are plenty of women, Mum." His thoughts jumped straight to Ava. *Hell no.* That had not been a date, and even if he noticed she'd grown into quite an attractive package since he'd last seen her, it was no matter. Thinking of Wyatt's younger sister like that was the last thing he planned on.

"How was your dinner?" he asked, hoping he sounded casual and changing the subject away from himself.

"You're not being subtle." She arched a fine brow. "I told you to stop mothering me. I'm fine."

He heaved in a breath but was happy to see a little spunk in her attitude. "Mum, I love you. I'm allowed to worry. When are you next going to the doctor? Is it Monday?"

"Actually, I cancelled my appointment."

"What? Why?" Connor shifted so he could look at his mum's face. Her eyes darted from his. "The doctor is worried. You're not eating enough."

"I am." A small sob sounded and Connor's stomach bottomed out. *Not the crying. Please, not the crying.*

"Mum." He gathered her close once more. He'd asked again in the morning. "Are Cassie and Clare home?"

His mum sniffled and broke away, but thankfully the tears seemed to have dried up. "Cassie is in her room studying. She studies too much that girl, just as bad as you about not having a life and balance. Clare went out to dinner with that new guy she's seeing."

Connor rolled his eyes. "You might be the only mum in the world complaining that her kids aren't all out getting up to mischief on a Friday night. You know we aren't all teenagers anymore." Not that he'd ever really felt like a teenager. At least not in the cutting loose and getting drunk every weekend kind. His eighteenth birthday had been spent beside his father's side in hospital, watching his mentor, idol, and best friend slip away from the world. Getting drunk had been the furthest thought from his mind.

He'd done plenty of that after. To numb the pain that never seemed to dissipate.

"I know, darling. I just want to see you happy. You're so focused on work and this new convention centre project. I barely see you smile these days."

Connor pulled his lips into a cheesy grin, showing every bit of his teeth he could. "Look. Smiling," he said through clenched teeth.

It did the trick. His mum let out a laugh. "You're such a joker. Just like your dad."

"C'mon. I feel like watching a movie," Connor said quickly. He couldn't bear to see the loss that still shadowed his mum's face whenever they mentioned his dad. Their loss had sent all of them into a spiral, but it had fallen to Connor to pick up the pieces and move them all along.

Fourteen years on and he was still holding them all together. That was just part of his life.

4

Connor stepped through the front glass doors of Gray Designs, shrugging his shoulders to adjust his backpack and let out the heat trapped there. He'd had to run to make his train after a rare sleep in. How the hell had he forgotten to set an alarm? Not the start he'd wanted for his Monday morning.

He flicked his gaze to the couch off to the side of the lobby, surprised to see Ava sitting there, writing notes in a notebook.

Changing direction away from the sleek lift area, he stopped just short of her high heels that appeared to be tapping out a beat.

"Ava?"

Her head shot up, eyes wide. "Oh, hey." She squinted and rubbed at her head.

"You didn't hit your head again, did you?"

She cocked her face to the side as she sent him a withering stare. "No. But thank you so much for the reminder. I'm just waiting for my swipe card. Apparently IT are on the job, but there was a miscommunication."

Connor raised a brow. That was rare, seeing as everyone

in the team was always on top of every little detail. He'd heard Brian say on Friday that he would personally take care of the details of Ava starting this morning.

"I'll take you up. You're sitting in my office since we'll be working closely."

Connor hadn't meant the frustration in his words.

"Try not to be so happy about that," Ava quipped, not missing his tone.

"Sorry. It's not you personally. I'm frustrated that Nexbo are making us jump through these hoops." He offered a half smile. "And I slept in so I'm late."

"Seems as though we're both off to a cracking Monday start then."

She stood, her shift hitting Connor with a wave of her perfume, stronger than it had been on Friday but still appealing. A subtle mixture of floral and vanilla. Her heels brought her up to his chin, and he noted she lifted her face a little at his study of her. What was that hanging from her ears?

"Are you quite done?" she snipped, ducking her head so their eyes met.

"You're in a snarky mood." He coughed, trying to cover up the fact something had distracted him. Her.

"You're staring at me as though I've grown three heads."

He was, he realised. Leaning in a little, he flicked a finger at her earrings. "Are you wearing pieces of cheese?"

"Yes. Swiss. Can we get to work now, please?"

He held up his hands. "Far be it from me to stall your brilliance."

They wandered over to the bank of lifts, and he pressed the button. He shoved his hands in his pant pockets and casually leaned against the wall. "Can I ask why you're wearing cheese slices at your ears?"

Ava hitched her laptop bag further up on her shoulder,

getting a little tangled with her handbag that was slung over the crook of her arm. "Because I like earrings."

"Right. May I?" Connor reached out and shifted her handbag, allowing her to move the laptop bag properly.

"Thanks. I'm allowed to like earrings, am I not?"

"Of course." The lift sounded its arrival with a ding before the doors slid apart, and Connor pushed off the wall, then held them open, ushering Ava inside.

Brian Gray stood at the back of the lift. His face slid into a bright smile when he saw them both. "Morning, how nice to see you both." His gaze flicked between the two.

Connor nodded. "Brian. I'm taking Ava up as she mentioned an IT issue."

"Oh yes. That's my fault. I forgot to ask them about her swipe card. Lucky you found her and have got it in hand." The older man's smile turned cheeky, and he lifted his hands in an oops gesture.

Connor locked his jaw. Just what was the old man up to? There was no way he'd forgotten. Brian Gray may not be an active part of the business like he used to be, but he was still sharp as a tack and made it his business to know everything that was going on.

"It's a pleasure to see you again," Ava chimed in. She threw Connor a dark look.

"It's our pleasure to have you as part of our team. I hear great things from Nexbo. I think you and Connor will make a perfect match."

Connor choked and tried to cover the gesture with a cough.

The lift stopped at the nineteenth floor and Brian stepped out. "Keep me up to date on how you get on," he said as he walked off.

The doors slid shut, silence taking over as the lift whooshed up another six floors.

"Was it just me or did Mr Gray seem a little odd then?" Ava said as they stepped out of the lift.

"Yeah, something seemed off. Don't call him Mr Gray either. He hates it. Apparently, it makes him feel old. This company is really like being part of a giant family. Anyway, my office is on this side of the building. This floor houses most of the senior architects. Miranda and Lucas are up two levels in the executive offices. Wyatt in on that floor too." He slid a sideways glance to Ava who grimaced but then seemed to pull herself together, straightening her shoulders.

"Did you speak to Wyatt over the weekend?" She forced the words out, as though she didn't want to ask but had to.

"We had a beer Saturday afternoon. And no, I said nothing."

Her gaze shot to his. "Really?"

"Yes, really. You asked me not to. If I make a promise, I keep it. Whilst I don't agree with this situation, and I hate lying by omission to my best friend, I know you two have shit to deal with. I just ask you don't leave me in the middle for too long."

"I won't. I will talk to him."

She nibbled her lip before flicking her gaze to him once more. "Why did you agree to this?"

Connor rolled her words over in his head, asking himself the same question. "I guess I always felt bad for you at school, you got a raw deal with being picked on. I've always wondered if maybe I could have helped a little more. You were so against me telling Wyatt anything back then. Maybe it's stuck." He shrugged.

"You have a hero complex."

He coughed. "What? No, I don't. I just don't like women getting a raw deal. If you need time to smooth over your past with Wyatt, then… okay. Just don't drag it out."

Connor rounded the corner and walked into his office.

The twenty-fifth floor was mostly open plan with long wooden tables that ran along one length of the building. Polished concrete floors echoed with the clip clop of Ava's heels and his own recently-shined leather shoes. Natural light flooded the space from floor-to-ceiling windows that inter-spaced the outer wall. Feature brickwork ran along the inside, the texture a nice offset to the smooth floors and exposed beams.

Giant indoor plants flashed vibrancy around the room, breaking up the urban and stark white space. He didn't know how the plants were always so healthy and, well, alive. Any attempts he'd made at indoor plants had ended in disaster and a trip to the compost.

"This is stunning," Ava said after spinning around and taking in the space.

"Yeah. It's quite a calming area. The office is glass-walled, so it's got great lighting, but if I need quiet, I can close the door which locks all outer sounds away." He waved to an empty desk that was set up against one wall. "That's you."

He'd had a couch in that spot that he'd shifted next to the door. He slept on it on the odd occasion he worked late and hadn't bothered to make the commute back to North Sydney where his mum's house was.

Ava glanced at him. "I can set up at the table out there if that's better for you? I don't want to be underfoot."

Connor shrugged. "We can work it out. Why don't I show you our current design and we can get started? I need to warn you though, I don't feel like there is much wriggle room."

Ava's mouth tilted upwards, but it would be a stretch to call it an actual smile. "I see."

* * *

Ava mentally stamped her foot. Hard. No, scrap that. She'd stamp her heel on his polished black leather arsehat shoes. Or maybe she'd knee Connor in the balls instead. That would certainly give her some satisfaction given the way he was acting.

They'd been there for barely an hour and already Ava could see she would not be able to do her job. Every word Connor spoke had cemented he was going to be as flexible as the polished concrete floors. The few times she'd tried to say anything, he'd shut her down, shushing her or waving a hand in her face.

"I need a coffee," Ava inserted into his latest monologue.

"Oh." Connor's eyes shot up, his focus landing on her for the first time since he'd dragged her over to his table that housed a large-scale drawing board and a miniature to-scale model of his proposed convention centre design. His brow furrowed. "Okay. There's a coffee cart on level two, or state-of-the-art machines are in the kitchen area on level nineteen."

Ava gritted her teeth at Connor's distraction. The man was a bloody machine with his work, and he certainly didn't stop to take a breath or consider other people's thoughts when he was in work mode.

It was an interesting side to him.

"Do you want anything? Coffee? Or maybe water to offset all those words you've spewed at me." She was snippy but didn't care. She was here to do a job, not be told to keep quiet and listen.

He levelled her with a look. "You seem annoyed."

"I am. You're treating me like an imbecile."

"An imbecile?"

"Yes." Ava fisted her hands and planted them on her hips. "I'm going to find some caffeine and water. Whilst I'm gone, I suggest you remember they have hired me to *assess* your designs and work *with* you as a team to get this design approved. You need my input if you want Nexbo to move further with the project. Because I can tell you now, for free, there is no way the government is going to approve the fantastical and over-the-top design you just pitched."

With one last huff in Connor's direction, she marched to the desk she'd been allocated to collect her bag. The bright cherry-red leather was stupidly calming, as though it held the answer to her decaffeinated world.

"Just wait a minute. You can't throw an accusation like that at me, then just stomp off. I've put hours into this design. Nexbo loved it when we presented it to them."

"Yes, and then they hired me."

The words flung into the large space, slowly seeping all the air from the room.

Connor's throat bobbed as he appeared to grasp for words to fling back. "Wait a minute…" Connor rubbed his ear. "You don't think they like it?"

He folded his bottom lip under, a tinge of something she couldn't quite place lighting his eyes. Hurt? She understood that the design was his baby, but this was a job. He needed to take a step back from his work and look at the bigger picture. Time to take a new strategy.

Ava dropped her handbag back on the desk and slumped on the edge. "I think they love it. Who wouldn't? It's amazing, Connor. But it's not a realistic sell in today's climate change aware environment. You need to think green. You're thinking big, but you need to remember this is now a government concern. Nexbo can't just approve a design because they love it. It's being built right on the harbour. It's replacing a building that's already functional to most people's standards. There needs to be a valid reason for *this* design to go ahead. Just because it's an amazing design doesn't mean the city needs it. You need to remember this is part of a revitalisation project, not a bid to win prestigious awards."

Connor picked up his mechanical pen and tapped it against the palm of his hand a few times. He then twisted it between his fingers.

Ava bit her lip at Connor's escalating tension, his shoulders locking, his jaw so tight she feared he might snap a tooth. He'd played rugby as a kid, as had Wyatt—just one of the many things about her brother she'd followed from a distance—but until now, she'd never really paid much attention to how big and burly Connor must have appeared on the field back then. His shoulder span really was quite impressive.

Not that she was noticing his physique.

Her mouth became arid, so she swallowed.

Clipped footsteps sounded from outside the open door, and a deep male voice called out Connor's name. Without sensible thought, Ava dived for Connor's large, wooden desk. She ducked down in front of his office chair and crawled into the small space, effectively hiding herself from anyone coming into the room.

"What the actual hell?" Connor muttered expletives and stepped around to the back of the desk, peering down at Ava.

"I can't let Wyatt see me," she whispered. "Not yet. Please?"

Connor cocked his head, then smirked.

"Connor?" the man said again as he entered the office.

Ava ducked down farther just as another set of polished leather shoes appeared at the doorway. These were worn with stark black pants. The base of the desk stopped her from seeing anything else.

Mending fences with her brother was something she desperately needed and wanted, but not now. Call her a coward, but she still hadn't worked out how she was going to go about regaining Wyatt's trust. Having him shut her out in this new work environment just wasn't something she could handle right now. She needed to make a good impression! A screaming match with her brother would not be her best start.

"Morning, *Lucas,*" Connor drawled.

Lucas? Oh, man, kill her now. Air whooshed from Ava's body. How had she not recognised Lucas's voice? Connor had, hence his shit-eating grin.

It wasn't her brother. It was the co-owner of the bloody company, and she'd just dived for the underside of Connor's desk as though she was re-enacting an action movie.

There was something seriously deranged about her today.

Just how the hell did she explain that one to Connor?

Cringing, she shuffled herself back from the desk a little, and turned her head only to meet eyes full of mirth before they pivoted back towards the door.

"Where's Ava?" Lucas asked. "Brian said he saw you two together this morning, and that you were making a start on the project. I wanted to check in with you both to see how it was going." Part of Ava died with embarrassment. It was bad enough Connor witnessing her random actions, and now she had to explain to the boss of the company she desperately wanted to impress, why she had a sudden urge to play hide and seek.

There was a weighty pause where Ava was pretty sure she shaved ten years off her life. Think... What could she possibly say? She'd dropped a pencil? *So lame...*

Perhaps a piece of paper floated under here? An important piece of paper.

Spilled water?

"Bathroom," Connor replied. "She went to the bathroom."

For the second time in as many minutes, Ava closed her eyes in relief.

"We're going to grab coffee and take a break. We can come up to you in about ten if you like?" Connor added.

"No need. I'm heading out for a meeting with a potential new client. I just thought I'd check in. Wyatt's out of the office all this week, isn't he?"

Ava's stomach rolled over, heat burning her cheeks.

"He sure is." Connor practically sing-songed.

Ava scrunched her nose; he could have mentioned *that*.

"I'm confused; why does that make you happy?"

Connor chuckled. "It doesn't."

"Right. I'll just leave that alone then."

Connor chuckled again. "Maybe I like the peace and quiet that comes with his absence."

This time Lucas chuckled. "Fair enough. Since Wyatt is on holiday, we'll wait to appraise him of the changes once he's back. I'll check in with you later. Tell Ava we're excited to have her on board. I've heard a lot of good things."

Lucas's footsteps receded, and Ava sank her forehead to the cool ground, trying to ignore she was essentially bowing her head where Connor's shoes would normally sit, as though she was worshipping the ground he walked on. Such a terrible image, and it didn't help her total state of embarrassment.

"Okaaaay. You can come out now. The big bad boss has left." Connor laughed.

The chair behind her shifted, though a quick look to her right revealed he still stood, propped against the edge of the desk, probably waiting to witness her embarrassing crawl back out of her idiocy.

Ava stood up, holding her head high, and ignored the neon bright red spots she knew flared in her cheeks.

"Thanks," she quipped, then took a step past him.

His hand shot out and grasped hers. "You want to explain why you had the sudden urge to imitate Bruce Willis?"

"No. I don't care to explain." Ava swallowed. Up close, the flecks of light that highlighted the amusement lurking in Connor's expression were quite magnetic. She could also smell that same appealing masculine scent he'd had Friday night, minus the sweaty aftertaste.

He wore a suit far too well.

"Pity, here was I hoping for a *'Yippee Ki Yay'*. Guess I better get you that caffeine before your Jackie Chan instincts kick in."

"You're not funny," Ava said, gritting her teeth to stop the smile that ached to cross her features.

"Come with me if you want to live," Connor replied in a terrible monotone Terminator accent.

"All right! You've made your point." Ava pushed at his shoulder, giving up her attempt to keep her humour at bay. "You're such an idiot."

Connor just grinned. "You gotta ask yourself one question…"

"Do I feel lucky?" they both said at once.

Ava burst into laughter. Connor did as well, his eyes crinkling at the corners in a way that made his eyes light up and sparkle. His broad shoulders shook, and he loosened the neck of his tie, pulling it out of the knot and throwing it over to the side of his laptop.

"You're into action flicks?" he asked with a lighter tone in his voice.

She struggled to keep her thoughts on their conversation and gave up. The breath left Ava momentarily, the change in Connor from studded-up workaholic to laid-back amusement, throwing her. He looked at ease as he unbuttoned the top of his shirt, and that one move left Ava squirming. She thanked her choice in a bra that had extra padding, the scratch of the fabric against her pebbled nipples only adding to the friction coursing through her body.

It threw her back to moments from her childhood, snap-shots of Connor from school, the golden-haired boy always wearing a smug and cocky grin. It only just hit her now how he'd changed. Back then, he'd had a carefree air about his persona that was missing. The glimpse of it now shocked something inside her.

"Ava?" Connor repeated, rubbing at his chin.

"Sorry?" she said, unable to remember what he'd asked.

"You like action movies?"

"Oh, yes. If I watch a movie, it's always an action flick. Or I read books."

"Action books?"

"Uh, sometimes," she prevaricated, not prepared to admit that truth. "You said coffee?"

He stared at her for another moment, then pursed his lips.

"Yes, I said coffee. Let's go grab some, and then maybe we could go for a walk. You can tell me more about your experience. You're right, I haven't exactly approached this the correct way."

Ava lifted one side of her mouth. "That sounds good. So Wyatt's out of the office for the entire week?"

"Yep. He's on holidays. Won't be in until next week. It's not likely he'll hear anything about you until then."

"Gee, thanks for telling me that earlier."

"Hey, you didn't ask. And I'm not getting involved, remember?"

She let out a deep huff, relief filling every inch of her chest. There was no need to stress about running into Wyatt for this week at least. Maybe working with Connor wouldn't be so bad if he could meet her halfway.

And if she could keep her thoughts firmly away from his body.

5

"Tell me what your chief complaint with my design is."

They walked along the footpath, heading towards Circular Quay. Cars queued beside them, stuck in a glut of traffic with roadworks stalling the flow. Nothing unusual for this end of Sydney's city at present. It made Connor glad he didn't drive to work. Public transport might be a little packed, but at least it was more reliable and time efficient than sitting in a car for hours on end.

Ava threw him a glance, the move sending her high pony-tail into a swing. A few strands had escaped from the band and were whipping at her face when she tried to take a sip of her coffee. She hooked them away with a finger.

Connor noted her dress was plain black, her fingers bare of any jewellery. It seemed the only dressy part of her outfit that stood out as unique were those random earrings. Compared to most of the other women he'd worked with she was quite staid and boring in her outfit choice, yet something about the total package was appealing.

Shit, man. Get it together.

"Well, for a start, your design is just too much. It's flamboyant and arrogant. I'm sure it will get you many write-ups in Architecture journals and maybe nab you an award or two, but at an initial guess, it's going to take at least seventy percent more metal and steel and construction than the average amount for the space it's covering. That's just wasteful. It's a convention centre, it's not a national monument such as the Harbour Bridge or Opera House that will bring in the tourists to see its structure. It's about being functional and serving the right purpose. I don't think that kind of imbalance is justified."

Connor gritted his teeth, partly because her words were the absolute truth, a fact he'd known from the first moment he'd put pencil to paper. But he'd justified that to himself.

This design wasn't just his.

That was the other part of his frustration. This design *wasn't* all his. It had been a joint project and a part of him couldn't—no, wouldn't—let that go. He'd made a promise. How dare Ava suggest he strip away parts of what made it so amazing?

He shoved his hand into his pocket, rubbing at the piece of folded up paper that lay in the depths. "You don't sugarcoat your words much, do you?"

"I'm not getting paid to appease your ego, Connor. I'm getting paid to ensure that Nexbo receive a design concept that fits their vision whilst also ticking all the environmental and sustainability boxes the government are going to throw their way. I want this to work as much as you do."

Connor sighed. "Lucas warned me that Nexbo were going to face issues with getting the design approved."

"Then why did he let you go forward with your current design? Surely he can see the same things I've said."

"He probably can, but this is my project. I landed the

contract. This is a design concept I've been refining for a while now." Connor didn't add the cliff notes version which tacked on it being a childhood vision.

"Okay." Ava nodded, as though she were running through a conversation in her head. "Let's get gelato."

Connor jolted, her shift in subject giving him verbal whiplash. "You just ate a cookie."

"So? Being cooped up makes me hungry. Besides, the gelato bar at the other end of Circular Quay has an affogato flavour that's to die for."

"Do you constantly think about food?"

"Yep. If there was a supermarket close by, I'd duck in there. Cheese would be really nice right now."

"Cheese?"

"Yep. I like cheese."

"I'm seeing that." He placed his hands in his pants pockets and playfully scoffed. "You're quite similar to your brother in some ways, do you know that?"

A subtle rouge tinged her cheeks, and she nibbled on her lower lip. The move drew his gaze. Something so innocent and yet he felt the kick to his libido seeing that little nip.

Her eyes flicked to his, her blue gaze hooded. "Do you think so?"

Connor cleared his throat, booting his inappropriate thoughts to the gutter where they belonged. "Yeah. Wyatt loves cheese and coffee and needs to eat constantly. He's also not afraid to say what he's thinking. He's not as big a klutz as you, but that's a high bar you set in that department."

"Gee, thanks," she fired back, but he could tell his words had pleased her.

As if on cue, she tripped over a piece of the pavement that had shifted because of a tree root. He reached a hand out to steady her, rolling his eyes in amusement but saying nothing.

They walked in silence for a bit more, Ava finishing the last sips of her coffee before she threw it into a rubbish bin.

He rubbed at his jaw, regretting his next words before they even left his mouth. "Why are things with you and Wyatt so bad? I know something happened years back, but I never got the full story. Only that he was livid with you. Then you disappeared off the face of the earth."

She pursed her lips, then scrunched her shoulders up to her ears before straightening them back down, as though she were preparing to take to the field for a big game or steadying her mind to present a paper to a room full of people. It was quite a show of preparation for something that should have been a simple answer to a simple question.

But life was never simple when it came to family.

"I screwed up. I did something that I really regret, like *really* regret, and it's taken me until now to work up the courage to ask Wyatt for forgiveness. There are circumstances I don't think he's aware of. Part of the situation I never knew until recently."

"The cryptic award of the year goes to Ava De Vere. Congratulations."

She sent a well-aimed elbow to his rib cage. "I know it's cryptic. But I think Wyatt needs to be the one to hear the full story first. Besides, you don't want to get involved, remember?"

"Touché."

She turned her face up to the sun and did a little spin. "You know there are ways to amend your design without completely losing the general concept. We just need to work through some alternatives."

The look of bliss and happiness that spread across her face distracted Connor, and it took a minute for her words to sink in. "Alternatives?"

"Sure. Things like utilising the sun. You could change

your roof design so that it's made entirely of skylights, and other forms of natural light. The sculptural aspect of your design could incorporate eye-catching panels that provide shade and maximise daylight as needed. You could even make them colourful. Interspersed with solar panels. With tweaks like that, and ensuring all interior lighting was LED, then you could almost power the entire building using those natural sources. That sort of thing wouldn't change the structure of your design much but would make it far more appealing on the sustainability front."

"I suppose," Connor said, intrigued by the idea despite his immediate need to deny any changes to the design. "It's a convention centre though, it's going to require a lot of electricity. Do you really think we could generate enough power? Plus, they require numerous theatres which require a night-time feel."

"Then change it up. Put the theatres in the basement."

Connor assumed this comment was flippant given the look Ava threw him.

"Utilise moving panels around the actual theatre floor that change with the sun, so that light is always blocked during the daytime while soaking in the sun's rays. At night you could open all the panels, giving fresh air and the allure of the night sky."

"That might be distracting, though. They said bold, not sustainable."

"They want both, you need to read the underlying message here, Connor. Push back on the areas that you need to maintain in your design but give them alternatives."

"Aren't you meant to be working for them?"

"Yes. But that doesn't mean I want you to lose, since you're clearly very passionate about your design. I'm a big believer in having my cake and eating it too."

They reached the gelato store and Connor turned to Ava. "Again with the food?"

She shrugged. "When in Rome…. Now, I'm going for the affogato, and cookies and cream. What are you having? It's my treat."

Connor shook his head. Who the hell was Ava? With every word she spoke, she became more interesting. One minute she's throwing herself under his desk at the thought of being discovered by her brother, and the next she's demanding he challenge his client.

One thing Connor knew, after only one day, he found himself enjoying her company, which left him with a serious problem.

* * *

Ava flopped face down onto her bed. Work had been… exhilarating. Working with Connor was far more enjoyable than she'd pegged. Plus, once he'd confirmed her brother was actually out of the office for the entire week, she'd calmed down and settled into the role she was being paid to do.

She knew she was good at her job.

Work was easy.

There were boundaries, and rules and numbers, and all things she could deal with. Where Ava always came unstuck was how to deal with the emotional issues in her life. What she needed was a plan on how to approach Wyatt—preferably outside of the office. Given the last words he'd said to her was he never wanted to see her again, and that was ten years ago, she hoped maybe he might have settled a little. *Or maybe not.*

That was part of the issue.

She had no idea how Wyatt was going to react to her

working at Gray Designs. And what's worse, she had no idea how he'd react to her working so closely with Connor.

That hadn't been her choice.

When Nexbo hired her, she wasn't told who she'd be working with, only that it was with an architect within Gray Designs. Would Wyatt believe that? Or would he just think she was manipulating things?

How those words had always stuck with her—his accusation of her manipulating the family.

Her supposed exploitation of their father paying her thousands of dollars, and only using that to string their father along. How she'd never followed through on any of her promises to spend time with them as a family.

Pfft. Like she'd had the chance to do that.

Ava had never seen a cent of that supposed money. Nor had she ever seen more than a four-worded card from her father.

All this so-called communication and monetary contribution had never come anywhere near her.

She rolled off the bed and moved in front of the top drawer of her dressing table before pulling out the envelope that lay beneath a pile of knickers. How different would her life have been if she'd discovered this earlier, not just a few months ago?

Finding out her mother—her own flesh and blood who was supposed to love her and protect her—was using her. She scoffed. Far too little. Far too late. The damage was well and truly done. Years ago.

Back then, she'd used her anger to drive herself out of the hellhole her mum had led her to and abandoned her in. It hadn't been easy, but she'd worked and put herself through her studies. She'd found her passion in sustainability and had worked hard to get where she was today.

But her interaction with her father and Wyatt had always haunted her.

The unsent half-written letter by her mother that she'd found had shone a new light on the situation.

Ava still did not know what had happened to her mother. Where she'd disappeared to or what she was doing with her life. Nor did Ava care. Her upbringing hadn't been ideal, but it made her stronger. She'd probably never get a genuine family like others took for granted, but she'd be damned if she'd not give her all at a chance at being a part of the Gray Designs family.

Work was truly worthy. Family was not.

Collecting her phone from where she'd thrown it on the bed, she went to her sent messages. The message to her father sat there. Had he read it? Was he still deciding whether to talk to her? Or had her actions at his wedding ruined any chance of that? No matter her pleading to justify her misaligned thoughts now.

They say to let bygones be bygones, but could she live with that? She'd never really forgiven herself for the way she'd acted out that day. Even in her rage she'd known she was doing the wrong thing. No one deserved to have their special day ruined. She'd paused on the threshold, seeing her father's face beyond happy. Wyatt had stood off to the side, an arm looped around a shiny-faced, pretty thing. It had been one snapshot of happiness after another, until Ava had barged in to tear it all down.

Because of lies. Lies she'd been fed. But what's worse, they were lies she'd believed.

Never again would she let herself care so much for another that she'd go against her principals.

* * *

Connor shifted the bags of groceries to one hand, using his other to unlock the front door of his mother's house. He'd left work early, purely with the purpose of wanting to get home in time to ensure his mum ate a balanced meal. Protein and vegetables, that was what the doctor ordered. His heart contracted, immediately jumping to the images in his mind from this time last year. Of her pale face and lifeless body lying on the kitchen floor. Images that were permanently engrained into his brain.

"Mum? Cassie? Clare?"

He moved through to the kitchen, dumping the bags on the counter. He took out the T-Bone steaks, placing them on the corner of the bench. Broccoli, carrots and potatoes came next. He'd boil them. Nothing exciting, but he wasn't aiming for a Michelin star. Just good solid food to ensure his mum didn't faint from not eating like last year. It had been the same every year, almost from the point his father had passed. During the lead up to the anniversary of his death, his mother would fall to pieces. But last year she'd taken it to a new level, having stopped eating to the point her body keeled over.

Sunday loomed like a black spot on his soul.

But this year he'd make sure she ate. No way was he having a repeat performance. That feeling of stark terror wasn't something he ever wanted to experience again.

"Hello, darling, you're home early," his mum announced as she walked into the room.

Connor frowned, surprised to see she was wearing black tailored pants and a nice blouse. "I'm here to cook you dinner."

"That's sweet, but I've eaten." Her eyes danced from his, taking in the array before her. "Maybe tomorrow night?" A pained expression filtered across her features before she wiped it clear, offering him an apologetic smile.

"You've eaten? It's only just gone six." Connor rotated his wrist to check the time, then he narrowed his gaze at his mother. Surely his mum would not lie about eating this year? Did he need to speak to her doctor again?

"I had dinner with a friend."

Connor snorted—his mum never went out.

"Which friend?" He tried to level the accusation in his tone, missing the mark if his mum's expression was anything to go by.

Cassie chose that moment to walk into the room. "Ooh, are you cooking?"

"Yes. Now, is Clare home? Maybe you can set the table for four."

"Yeah, she's in her room."

"You don't need to set a place for me, I've eaten. Though your brother appears to have a hard time hearing that for some reason. I'll sit with you all, though. I bought a nice cabernet on my way home; it will go nicely with your steak. I'll just enjoy a glass of that whilst you all eat."

Connor stared at the woman before him. She still looked like his mum, even wearing nicer clothes than her usual practical shorts and T-shirt. But he was having a hard time following her words.

"Mum, you can't stop eating."

Cassie's brows rose then fell as she threw Connor a warning glance. Too bad. He would not walk on eggshells around his mother and allow a repeat performance of last year.

"Connor, I don't think we need to re-hash—"

"Cassie, honey," his mum interrupted. "Thank you, but it's fine. Connor, I appreciate your concern, but I have already eaten. I am still your mother. You can stop treating me like a child."

"Then you can stop acting like one. I'll make you a small

plate." Connor nodded, his mum would thank him, eventually. She needed to eat. Lying about the situation was just childish.

He picked up the steaks and walked outside to turn on the barbecue, missing the silent exchange of glances his mum and sister shared.

6

By Wednesday, Connor felt as though he and Ava had reached a good vibe with their working habits. The design was still undergoing tweaks, but he could see where Ava was coming from. Instead of burying his head in the sand around his design, he had read some articles she'd sent him, and he'd spoken to some other designers who were focusing more on the green space. He was doing his best to shift his vision, fighting against the desire to outright refuse any changes. He was in control of his work situation. That was what mattered.

Wyatt had sent him pictures of his week away, enough to give him heartburn. His mate had asked how the design was going, and though Connor had tapped out a response with a brief explanation of his work with Ava, at the last minute he'd deleted her name.

Unfortunately, whilst his working life seemed to level out with this latest change, his home life wasn't.

The weekend was looming and he could feel the tension mounting at home.

Of course they were all still affected, but he and his sisters were moving on. They didn't give up on living like his mum seemed to whenever the anniversary rolled around.

Pulling out his phone, he texted Cassie who he'd asked to study from home today, needing someone to monitor their mum. She'd sat at the table with them during dinner last night, but true to her word, she'd refused to eat a bite. Connor was tied up in knots over what to do.

Connor: Is mum up yet? Can you check on her?

It didn't take long for Cassie's reply to come through.

Cassie: Mum woke and left the house right after you this morning. She's not back yet.

Not back yet? He flicked a look at this watch. It was after two o'clock. What the hell? Did he need to go look for her? His mother never went out. Where the hell had she gone? This week of all weeks? His skin crawled, as though tiny ants marched up his spine. What if something had happened to her?

A sick dread spread through him at that thought.

"Connor? You're going to snap that pencil if you keep that up," Ava stated with a pointed glance at his hand.

"My mum's missing," he blurted.

"Missing?" Ava's brows furrowed.

"Yeah. She left home this morning and hasn't been seen since."

Ava cocked her head to the side and squinted at him a little. "Okay. Have you called her?"

Called her. Why hadn't he thought of that? He shook his head, reaching for his phone. Clicking on his recent calls, his mum's name came up within his list. There weren't a lot of numbers on there, to be honest. His mum, Clare, Cassie, Lucas, Miranda and Wyatt. And Ava's name was now on that list.

So his life was mainly all about work. That didn't make him a workaholic.

The phone connected after three short rings, his mother's voice chipper on the other end.

"Hello, darling, to what do I owe this pleasure?"

"You're okay?" Thrown by the lightness of her tone, he ignored her question.

"Of course. I had some errands to run this morning and have just stopped for coffee and some lunch."

"Why didn't you tell Cassie where you were going?"

"She was studying. I popped my head in and said I was going out and would be back later."

"You never go out."

Ava's head popped up when he spoke, her wide eyed stare cluing him into the fact he probably shouldn't have said it, a fact confirmed when his mother's voice frosted over.

"Connor, I am a grown woman and am entitled to do as I please. Perhaps instead of spending all your time and energy watching over me, you could find yourself a life."

She hung up.

Pulling the phone from his ear, he looked at the screen, as though an alien entity had taken over.

"So your mum's not missing." Ava still wore the same look she had earlier. It reminded him a little of the way people looked when they trod in dog poo.

"No."

"Connor, don't get angry, but why did you jump to the conclusion that something was wrong with your mum?"

"I... Well... She had a few fainting spells last year. She wasn't eating properly. It gave us all a scare."

"So now whenever she leaves the house on a whim, you immediately think she's missing?"

"You're making me sound like a deranged son. I'm just worried about her."

Ava nodded, the corner of her mouth lifting. She assessed him for a moment longer before returning to her work.

Okay. So maybe he'd overreacted to his mother's impromptu trip. But she was different this week. Not in the way she had acted in previous years. Which was good? He didn't want to see her sleeping the days away and avoiding going out. But he wasn't enjoying this version either. She seemed... annoyed at him. Or frustrated?

Hell, he didn't know. Maybe he was imagining things.

There was just a part of him that couldn't let go of his mother's face last year. He'd apologise tonight.

* * *

"How about vertical gardens? And vertical wind turbines? You could use the turbines to help with the electricity production." Ava leaned over Connor's shoulder and pointed to the various spots on his design that she was talking about.

It was Thursday afternoon, and though the past few days of working together and tossing around ideas had seemed to go okay, today it was not.

"It will end up looking like it's a building covered in plants."

"You make that sound like a bad thing?" Ava tried hard not to let her frustration show.

Connor had been receptive to new suggestions, and yet today it was as though he'd undergone a polar change.

Nothing she suggested was getting through. If anything,

he was backtracking and trying to return to his original design, eliminating any of the changes they'd incorporated. She was fed up with the mood changes.

"This design emulates aspects of the bridge and Opera house. If I put moss all over it, it's going to lose that link. I'm thinking big here, Ava."

Ava gritted her teeth. "I'm not suggesting moss. Jeez, what is wrong with you today?"

"Nothing," he spat. The muscles in his neck flexed as he appeared to be playing out a few things in his mind.

Instead of pushing him to talk, Ava walked to her desk and sat behind her laptop. If Connor wanted to be a dick about the project today, then she'd leave him to it. They clearly weren't going to make any progress with him in this mood.

She brought up a few articles she'd been reading the evening before, covering topics such as sustainability, green design and the difficulty in finding the perfect balance. Ava let out a soft snort. The resounding opinion was that green design was ugly, an opinion that really bugged her.

Green design doesn't have to be ugly, it just needs creativity.

Connor taped his pencil against his blueprint for a few beats. The tapping grated against her nerves, but something in his face stopped her from mentioning it. His eyes were bleak, almost a haunted expression in their depths.

He shoved his hand into his pants pocket and drew out a piece of paper. It was folded many times over and had the sort of deeper shaded crease marks that left Ava wondering just how often he looked at it.

And what was on it?

Connor looked at the paper, turning it around in his fingers before he slowly opened it. The process mesmerised Ava, as though what he was looking at held some sort of reverence.

Whatever it was, it seemed to be priceless to Connor.

He laid it out over his design. From where she sat, Ava could make out a sketch. It was rough and appeared hand drawn. There were lines everywhere, scribbles of writing and loads of smudge marks.

Dragging her gaze from the piece of paper, Ava looked at Connor's face. Pain radiated from his every pore; his eyes so shadowed they imitated an inky-black sky. Tension pulled his shoulders and chest taut, his shirt stretching tight across his body. He placed both hands on the sides of the drawing board and bowed his head, his eyes never leaving the design.

Defeat. That was what he looked like. He looked a picture of defeat.

But why?

Ava was desperate to know. The strength of her feelings and concern towards him surprised her. She barely knew this Connor, not that she'd known him any better when they'd been younger. But even back then, he'd always had this untouchable confidence and dazzle about him.

Seeing him just now, it broke something inside her.

What had made him like this?

A part of her wanted to reach out, to ask, but that same part of her held back. She wanted *him* to come to her, for him to want to tell her what this was all about.

It didn't feel right her pushing him on this matter.

He stood, suddenly, his gaze flicking to hers.

Busted.

She glanced away, but not before the despair in his eyes deepened.

Footsteps against the polished concrete grew closer before the slip of paper floated across her keyboard.

"This was my father's." Connor stated. "He and I were working on it together. It was *our* dream, *our* secret project. And then he died." He swallowed.

Ava sucked in air, trying and failing to still the rapid beat of her heart. She knew he'd lost his dad, that the ramifications were still, and always would be, there. But this was on another level. The loss, fresh and strong, haunted him, as though it happened only yesterday. Her chest ached, wanting to reach out and lock Connor in her arms. To offer to siphon off his pain.

Looking at the design, so many things clicked into place. It may not have been obvious to everyone but having worked so closely with Connor these past few days, she could see exactly where the inspiration for his convention centre design came from.

"This is why you don't want to change things," she whispered.

"My dad's name was Cameron. It was a bit of a family in-joke. We were the five C's. He was the best dad. I know lots of people say that, but he really was. He worked hard but always made time for every one of us. He and Mum were so in love, it was kind of sickening. They were childhood sweethearts, married straight out of school, and I was born almost nine months to the day after their wedding. We had the sort of family connection and happiness you see in the movies. It was all too good to be true."

"What happened?" Ava asked, desperate to keep Connor talking.

"The big C. It's ironic, really. In a sick, twisted humorous sort of way." Connor huffed, a forlorn expression flashed briefly across his face. "He never lost his smile, or hope. At first when we found out, he went through treatment and we were told he'd have years. There was a strong chance he'd go into remission. We celebrated that day, so sure it was all going to be fine. Anything we asked for, we got. Ice cream for breakfast, pizza for dinner, and we all stayed up until midnight watching action movies because they were his favourite. Two months later he died."

"Connor—"

"Please don't. I don't want sympathy or condolences. I've had enough of that." His voice was stilted, his movements rigid as he reached out and fingered the corner of the design. "This was what he and I did when he went back into the hospital, when they told us it was more aggressive than they'd first thought."

Ava reached out and took Connor's hand. It was strangely cold, yet that one connection helped her see exactly where Connor was coming from.

"You want to honour him through his design."

Connor's head jerked up, his eyes going wide as they landed on her. "Yes," he murmured, surprise lacing the one word.

Ava squeezed his hand, staring at his face. Every one of his features called to her, and she drank them in. From his clear blue gaze to the slightly crooked slant of his nose. His mouth had pulled up at one end, his strong jawline covered in day-old stubble. Her fingers itched to run along that jaw, feel each bristle under the pad of her thumb. He'd discarded his tie around mid-morning again today, as seemed to be his habit. The top button of his stark white shirt was open, giving her a small glimpse of tanned, muscled skin that held a sparse covering of hair.

She dragged in a breath, having forgotten to breathe. Tingles spread from where her palm melded to his, as though a line was being drawn along her arm, lifting every hair in its wake. She swallowed, needing to bring any form of moisture to her mouth.

What was this?

Her eyes continued their path downwards, hopping from

one button to the next until she stopped, her gaze held forward. *Do not look any farther down, Ava.*

The urge to do so propelled her into a standing position. At a loss and needing to shake these phantom feelings off, she skirted her desk and threw her arms around Connor's neck and gave him a hug, except that only made the situation worse!

The connection shifted, an unfamiliar tension hung in the air.

Brought into full body contact, she was immediately aware of just how turned on she was by Connor's proximity. And he was equally so, if the sizeable bulge against her thigh was any sign.

Her nipples crushed against his hard chest, aching to feel skin-on-skin contact. His warmth was so welcome, not that it was cold by any means. She was about to break away when his arms came around her, crushing her to him. She drank in his scent, her nose slotting nicely against the apex of his neck and shoulder. A strong desire took over to rub her cheek along this spot and run her tongue along the hollow patch of skin, tasting him.

Oh, sweet Jesus, she was so toast.

This close, his heartbeat sounded through her, each thud a welcome vibration against her chest. She was attracted to Connor Linton. But what was worse was how connected to him she felt, as though she knew the real him, and that meant she could fall for him.

Did she want that?

Her head screamed no. Falling for Connor would be a further complication towards mending the gap with Wyatt. She was finally close to a point where she might actually achieve that goal. Any sort of dalliance with Connor would ruin that progress. Not to mention her job!

For that reason alone, she stepped back. She offered a

weak smile, avoiding the confusion she glimpsed in Connor's eyes.

She laced her arms across her chest, praying the silk of her camisole wasn't a dead giveaway of her aroused state. *Think, Ava. Say something before this gets awkward.*

"Your dad's design is amazing. We will do it justice. I promise."

And she meant every word.

How she'd work closely with Connor and not allow her body's reaction to deepen to him was another matter entirely.

7

You are not attracted to Ava De Vere
You do not have a 'thing' for her.
You do not want to have sex with her.

Connor repeated his mantra as his feet thudded against the pavement. Yesterday had been intense.

Why the hell had he shown Ava, of all people, that design? He'd not even showed his mum or sisters the sketch he'd worked on with his father.

Somehow it had become the one thing he had with his father that he'd never shared with anyone else. It was his good luck charm, what he held absolutely precious.

And he'd shoved it in front of Ava as though it was the proof he needed to get his own way.

He never should have done that.

It had broken down one barrier he had for this job with her. Now she was going out of her way to make suggestions that worked within the confines of his design, because she knew its origin. And its meaning to him.

What had happened to his plan to not get involved?

He just wanted this job done. Signed off and settled. He

didn't want to get to know Ava, not the way his body was urging him to.

Yesterday he'd been in such a shitty mood, which should have been a sign for him to not go in. He'd taken out his frustration on Ava, and instead of fighting him she'd given him space, which had left him needing to justify his position—the exact thing his dad used to do when Connor was in a funk.

A bike whizzed past, and the rider yelled something at Connor. Bringing his flat-out run back to a jog, he panted, dragging in air too sparse.

He stepped off the path and walked towards the water. Last night he'd struggled to sleep. Images of Ava—naked and writhing—had featured highly, taunting him into some pretty hot and heavy dreams. He'd woken at five, a hot mess and horny as hell. Instead of taking a shower and dealing with the problem himself, which would have been his answer in the past, he decided on a run. He couldn't go into the office early, as his space there only made him think of Ava. Jerking off to thoughts of her was crossing a line.

Shit.

He'd been so close to kissing her yesterday. And damned if she wasn't exactly on the page with him. He had seen it in her eyes; her desire for him.

Which left them with a serious problem.

He flopped down on the grass, hooking his hands over his knees as he took in the water before him. The wind whipped up, creating crests of white across the rippled surface. He ran a hand through his hair, dragging at the tips.

Wyatt was due back this weekend. He'd texted yesterday morning, saying he and Evette had exciting news to share. That had been part of what had set off his shitty mood. The predicament of working so closely with Ava, but not having told Wyatt. Now his mate was engaged, and Connor could only predict that whole situation would end in disaster. His mum was acting… different. He was just waiting for her to fall apart. In the space of not even a week, so much shit in his life was changing, and it left with him with a sense of heartburn. He raked another hand through his hair.

How the hell did he justify lying to Wyatt?

He knew enough about his mate to know Wyatt despised lying.

Which was exactly what Connor was doing.

Not only had he not told Wyatt, but he'd also sided with Ava to give her time to speak to him. He was beginning to like her. Wyatt had written off the fact he even had a sister now. He didn't know the exact details, and he'd never asked.

Never wanted to, until now.

Just what the hell had happened between Ava and Wyatt? Their family situation was complex, and he'd never wanted to know why before. He had enough complexity in his own life.

He'd had two days of being eighteen when his dad had passed away. From that point on, his life had become all about survival, about keeping his mum from falling any further into the depths of despair she'd already delved into. She'd barely left her room, hell her bed, for that first year. His sisters had been so young. They were all so broken, but he'd been the only one to keep it together.

He'd stepped up and taken over as the man of the house—he'd had to.

Connor had learned to cook, and to clean. He'd deferred his study for that first year, put aside his plans to travel the world and find out what made him tick, to be there for his mum and sisters.

He'd worked two different jobs, and not once had he regretted those decisions, because whilst his mum hadn't been able to function, he knew he was the opposite. If he stopped for too long, he'd fall apart.

And he'd never stopped from that moment.

Doing things and being active kept him sane. Focussing on his mum and sisters, studying, and now his work is how he has kept his life stable and happy.

Inserting a seriously complicated woman into that mix would not end well.

He had enough issues on his plate. This week in particular. His mum had done another one of her personality switch-a-roos last night, telling him after dinner that she was going to the movies with a friend.

Connor didn't even know his mum still had friends.

He thumped a hand down against the grass. He'd hoped a punishing run would help still the swirl of thoughts that refused to let him be, but so far it hadn't.

Maybe he just hadn't run far enough.

After dragging himself to a standing position, he jogged back to the path before pushing his body to its limits—sprinting interspersed with lighter jogging. He just needed to compartmentalise. There was always a way to deal with any issue thrown at him. All he had to do was focus.

By the time he arrived home he was dripping with more fluid than filled the Sydney Harbour. Every part of him ached, his body crying out for a hot shower or more preferably a soft couch to break his crumple to the floor. He hauled himself through the front door of his family home, deciding that being alone in his own studio would not help.

Besides, he needed to see how his mum was getting on.

"Mum? Cassie?" he called out, dropping his keys into the glass bowl at the front door. He plucked his wireless ear plugs out, casually tossing them on the entry table along with his phone.

The news reporter's monotone voice droned from a distance, but Connor couldn't hear people moving about.

Walking along the hallway, he poked his head into the lounge room. The TV was on but streaming to an empty room.

Would Clare be home? She'd been putting in crazy hours as a registrar at the Sydney Women's hospital and had recently rented a place with a few of her colleagues. Sometimes she'd pop in to stay here if she wanted a 'true' break from her medical life as she deemed it, but he hadn't seen her for a few days.

Continuing to the kitchen, he paused on the threshold. Clare was staring at a pot of tea, as though it held the answers to world peace.

"Hey," Connor said, propping his shoulder against the door frame.

Her brows rose a little before she slowly dragged her gaze away, turning towards him. She scrunched her nose and floated her eyes to his shoes and back up. "Have you taken up marathon training?"

"No." Connor pushed away from the panels. "Does that teapot perhaps mean you've just boiled the kettle?" he continued hopefully.

Clare pulled her mouth to the side, then turned and looked at the kitchen clock before swinging back to him. "Probably ten minutes ago." She leaned over the benchtop to flick the switch on the kettle.

"You've been staring at a teapot for ten minutes? Is that some part of your psychology major? Maybe a new technique you're leaning to assess clients' mental states?"

"Connor, you are not funny. I know that's going to come as a shock, but it's the truth."

Connor clutched at his heart. "The truth hurts," he replied with a sigh. "So why *are* you staring at the teapot?"

"Mum…"

The breath seized in his throat, an ache taking hold deep inside his chest. He struggled to move his slack limbs, their immobility nothing to do with the punishing exercise he'd just finished.

"The countdown is on." His words were solemn. "I keep waiting for her to get her look. Guess it will happen tonight. She's been so odd the past week."

It was the same every year. The lead-up to the anniversary of the day they had lost him. It never changed, though part of Connor really hoped it would. Every. Single. Year.

Not that he didn't feel the grief still. He missed his father like no tomorrow, but his mum had never moved on. Fourteen years later and he was still propping everyone up.

Abandoning the idea of coffee, he instead slumped onto one of the bar stools at the end of the kitchen bench. He'd been waiting for his mum to start her slide. That was the other reason he'd been so on edge yesterday, because the anniversary was Sunday and his mum was… He didn't want to say perky, but she hadn't fallen in her heap. Something about that unnerved him. Last night she'd gone out of her way to track him down and prove she was eating dinner. He'd frowned, and she'd told him to lighten up.

If he wasn't so under the pump at work, he'd have taken the day off to check she wasn't falling apart differently this year. Maybe going through a mental break or something?

Clare poured two cups of tea, methodically adding a dash of milk before bringing both to where he sat. She slid the cup in front of him.

"What do you want to do this year? I can pick up some flowers. There's a local place near the university that has the most gorgeous bundles of freesias and gerberas. I know work is really busy for you right now, so I can do that at least."

Connor shifted his gaze from the milky brown liquid before him to his sister. "No. I am busy, but never too busy for this. You have practical work coming up and you need to focus on that. I'll ring the florist on my way into the office and place our usual order. You know we always take yellow roses."

Clare looked at him for a beat, her lips pressed together in a slight grimace, then took a sip of her tea, wincing as she swallowed. Connor reached out and dipped a finger in the liquid. It was lukewarm.

"You don't always have to do everything, Connor."

His heart arrested at his sister's words, like another twist of a bolt applied to his chest. "I don't see it as doing everything," he shot back, cringing internally at the bite in his voice.

"Really?" Clare laid a hand on his shoulder and squeezed. "You held us together when dad died. I suppose I'm only realising now just how much, and how much you still do. But I'm also worrying it's at the jeopardy of your own life."

"Don't psychoanalyse me, Clare. I'm fine. Let's just get through this next week."

She opened her mouth to say something else but snapped it shut. A glimmer of hurt lurked in those depths, but Connor blanked his feelings. There was enough shit on his plate right now. He didn't want to go into any in-depth conversations with his sister about the sacrifices he'd made in his life. He'd done what he had to and didn't regret one single moment.

"I gotta go." He pushed away from the bench and walked out of the kitchen, along the hallway, and outside through the laundry. A hot shower and his sanctuary awaited. So what if he was a thirty-two-year-old guy who technically still lived at home? Once Clare and Cassie finished with their studies, he'd look to move. Maybe a place closer to the city.

Until then, someone needed to monitor them and his mum.

Especially his mum.

* * *

Ava pushed her notebook a little to the left, doing her best to pay attention to Lucas Knight. The man half owned the company; you'd think that alone would pull her thoughts into gear.

Her gaze travelled across the table to the end of Connor's tie. It was a gunmetal silver with a diagonal stripe woven into the fabric. She followed the pattern upwards, jumping from each line to the next until she reached the knot at the base of Connor's neck. He swallowed.

Was he itching to shed his tie? She took a surreptitious glance at her watch. Yep. It was about this time each day he'd normally be aiming to shed his tie.

He appeared entirely focused on Lucas, but she could tell he wasn't comfortable. He was twisting his pen between his fingers, a move he did whenever frustrated. Or was that just his tell-tale action for his irritation with her?

"Ava."

She startled, followed by an eerie ringing in her ear. *Shit. What were they talking about?*

"Yes," she replied, swinging to face Lucas.

His deep eyes scrutinised her, giving nothing away of whatever emotion he was feeling. Dammit. Was she in trouble already? She was meant to be making a great impression, not assessing the likelihood of Connor shedding his bloody tie, and his emotional state.

Lucas let out a chuckle. "I asked how you feel the design is going? How you think Nexbo will take these changes?"

"Uh, well…" Ava looked at the blueprints before her. Scribbled notes spread across the top right section, some hers and some Connor's. They'd been going back and forth on most of the suggestions that Ava had presented. "I think we have work to do still." She swallowed, daring a furtive glance towards Connor.

He was looking past them, seemingly at nothing. She turned her head a fraction, to see if someone was standing behind them, but there was no one. Nothing but the floor-to-ceiling glass window that showcased a picture-perfect blue sky.

She turned back to Lucas. He pursed his lips, looking at Connor then back to her. Slowly, his gaze shifted to the papers spread out on the wooden table before them.

"I'm going to be honest, I'd have thought you two would have made more progress than this."

Ava flicked a look at Connor. He was still staring at whatever was behind them.

"That's my fault," Ava blurted. "I'm still coming up to speed on the plans so far."

Which wasn't the truth, but Ava felt she owed it to Connor to cover for whatever distraction he was going through.

"I see," Lucas murmured. His lips tightened a little, and the pit in Ava's stomach widened. So much for showing her amazing skills, hoping to secure a full-time job here. So far all she'd done was impersonate action movies and argue with Connor.

"I have some ideas. There's a project I worked on down South that I think can be useful for both Connor and I to look at. I'll schedule that in. We are a little behind right now, but I promise we'll be on track for the meeting with Nexbo in two weeks' time."

Connor may as well have been asleep for all he was contributing right now. What the hell was wrong with him?

Lucas shifted in his seat and flipped shut the leather cover of his planner, signalling he'd heard enough. "I don't need to remind either of you of how important this project is to Gray

Designs. I'm sure you have it in hand." He nodded to them both, then with a slick of his hand to smooth his tie, he stood, collected his planner, and left the meeting area.

Silence took his place, infiltrating with a heaviness that sat square on Ava's shoulders. Had that been Lucas giving them a warning? Or was he stating a fact? Maybe a reminder?

She honestly couldn't tell from the matter-of-fact tone he'd used. But she'd bet every last cent of her savings that Lucas hadn't missed the fact they were both distracted.

Connor tipped his head back, cupping his hands around his head, and let out a huff. "Dammit."

"We need to get on the same page." Ava folded her hands together in front of her. She locked her shoulders, waiting for Connor to fly back with some angry or annoying response.

"I gotta make a call," he muttered before standing and moving back to his office.

Of all the? Ava opened then closed her mouth. Honestly, what the hell was up with him?

Before she could shift, her phone pinged. Stabbing at the screen, she opened the message without sending the phone spinning away.

Unknown: Ava, this is your father. Thank you for the message and for reaching out two weeks ago. Please accept my apologies for the delay in responding. I have been away on holidays and didn't want to reply until I was back in Australia. I would very much enjoy meeting for a coffee. Let me know what suits you.

· · ·

Her breathing shallowed, more of a pant than actually sucking in air. She'd sent that message and had written off any thought of getting a response. She oscillated between absolute euphoria and terror.

Finally.

Finally, she would get a chance to right the injustice of her childhood.

Did she reply right away? Or wait? She didn't want to wait too long, in case he changed his mind. But if she replied too quickly, would he think she was desperate?

Would that be far from the truth?

Lunchtime. She would wait an hour and reply then.

Her head spun as she dragged herself to a standing position and followed Connor. A goofy expression split her face, and she felt a little lightheaded.

Entering his office, she jumped as he slammed a fist down on the desk.

"Dammit!" Connor blurted. He slapped his hand down again and then bowed his head, dropping it between both hands.

Ava's heart flopped over and all thoughts of her dad vanished from her mind. "Hey, are you okay?" She rushed to his side, laying a hand against his upper arm. The muscle bunched, and warmth shot up the entirety of her right side.

"I need to find yellow roses. You'd think that would be easy? But no. Because I forgot to order them last week—like I normally do—my florist doesn't have any."

Ava frowned. She was not expecting that, but okay. "Um, how about trying another florist?"

He turned a droll look upon her. "I've tried four. The last just said there's a wedding on, which has sucked up a lot of stock around Sydney. Apparently the florist who had the order had some disaster, so they are buying up all the yellow roses to fulfil their order. Seriously. Of all the ruddy colours." He bowed his head again, shaking it from side to side.

The fabric stretched taut across his back muscles, the thin fabric doing nothing to hide their strength and breadth.

"Do they have to be yellow?" Ava asked, confusion lacing her words. She ripped her gaze off his back, ignoring the tingling in her fingers. They ached to slide across from his arm and massage the tension in those shoulders. Gingerly, she pulled her hand away and tucked it under her other arm.

"Yes!" Connor sprang to a standing position, energy vibrating with each rigid movement he made. He stalked around her, over to the other side of the room. He picked up a pencil and scratched a few notes on his drawing board.

"Why?" She stilled, watching each erratic move he made. She had no idea why, but not being able to track down yellow roses was bringing Connor undone before her.

He flicked a quick look her way, his eyes nothing short of black pools of pain—so far from his usual light and carefree persona.

It threw her into taking a step back.

The only sound in the room was the occasional scratch of his pencil against paper, but Ava stood her ground. Connor was hurting, and she wanted to know why.

No, she *needed* to.

He was making her personal life easier by not spilling her working situation to Wyatt. The least she could do was try to help him with his own personal issues. Because his misery told her this was very personal and very important.

"Connor. Talk to me. I'm here."

Her words snapped something inside him. He tossed the pencil onto his desk, then stalked across the room to flop onto the couch. "I need them for my mum. She always takes yellow roses to my father's grave."

8

"Let me a make a call."

Connor lifted the arm he'd flung across his face, watching Ava as she fossicked in her bag before pulling out her mobile phone. She tapped out a few numbers before walking out of the office; he supposed to talk to whoever she was calling.

Like it mattered.

The last florist had been pretty adamant he would not have any luck finding yellow roses. Like Ava, she questioned his requirement for yellow, offering any number of other colours. Help had been her only agenda, yet all Connor could do was grapple with anger and despair.

How could he have forgotten the roses? It was a tradition, an event that meant more to his mum and sisters than anything, yet this year he'd forgotten.

No, not forgotten. He was distracted. By the five-foot-eight doe-eyed, vibrant, glossy-haired, *definitely* off-limits woman now sauntering back into the office towards him. Why the hell was she grinning like that? It made her eyes pop and her lips spread in a way that made him want to kiss that expression right off her face until all she could do was whimper his name.

Nice plan, Connor. 'Cause that won't cause a complete shit storm with Wyatt.

"We can pick them up in the morning," Ava stated, her grin not budging a millimetre. And why should it? She had no idea where his thoughts had gone.

Her body flopped onto the couch beside him, closer than he'd have liked. Her warmth was like a beacon, and it was all he could do not to haul her onto his lap. What the hell was wrong with him? Distracted in meetings with the boss. Forgetting crucial tasks for his mum. Now lusting after his best mate's estranged younger sister?

"Connor?"

He turned his face, struck by the clear piercing blue gaze that met his.

"Did you hear me?" Ava continued, a small pucker of skin appearing between her brows.

He reached out and smoothed the small patch, her skin irresistible. Her eyes went wide and flickered to his mouth before shooting back up to meet his gaze. Something rumbled deep inside him, a shift he couldn't stop.

He moved, leaning in a little, but her quick gasp brought him up short.

Now was not the time, or the place. He was a mental wreck. Kissing Ava De Vere in his office at work would not add to that picture. Instead, he pushed himself to a standing position, then stalked to his desk and took a seat there, hoping the wooden top would give him time to calm other overjoyed parts of his body.

"Tomorrow morning?" He cleared his throat. "Where from?"

"From the flower markets at Homebush. A friend works there. She called in a favour. That last florist you spoke to wasn't wrong; there's a celebrity wedding on tomorrow that's bought up almost all the stock of yellow roses in New South Wales. It's crazy. But all good. We've found some."

Her voice was a little clipped, a smile plastered to her face, as though she were putting on a front and hiding her genuine feelings. He could relate. He sensed her puzzlement over his behaviour, as she should be. Hell, he had no idea what on earth he was doing at the moment? His mind was a spinning top, about to fly off the edge of the table and free-fall into nothing.

"Thank you." Connor swallowed, trying to dislodge the lump that had formed in his throat. "If you give me your friends' details, I'll go first thing to collect them."

Ava twisted the corner of her mouth, a small glimpse of white teeth folding her lip under. "We, uh, could go together?"

Why did those few words send his heart into a staccato beat within his chest? She was looking straight at him, her expression oscillating between hopeful and neutral.

"Sure," Connor blurted before he could monitor his response.

The knot loosened and his breathing came easier. He refused to analyse why that was the case.

"They open at five."

"A.M.?" he clarified.

"I'm afraid so." She let out a faint laugh, one he'd become used to hearing during their working hours together. It was always soft, and feminine, and left him feeling a little lighter.

"You make the coffee and I'll drive."

"Deal." She stood and walked to his desk, her hand held out to him.

He slid his larger palm against the smooth skin, unable to resist the urge to rub his thumb against the side of her hand.

Her cheeks bloomed with heat, and all he wanted to do was pull her over his desk and kiss her senseless.

"We'd better get these plans sorted," he choked out and snatched his hand back.

Work. Yep. Shit.

* * *

A solid wave of differing floral scents hit Ava as they walked through the main entrance. The flower markets, even at the ludicrous time of five-thirty in the morning, were a hive of activity. Voices rose and fell, shouts and requests flinging about in the air. The energy was amazing. She grabbed Connor's hand and dragged him farther inside.

She ignored the tingling their touch brought on, telling herself the only reason she took his hand was because it was really busy and he was her ride home.

Keep telling yourself that.

Her inner voice could be annoyingly on point sometimes.

Part of her had assumed Connor would pull said hand away, but to her surprise he threw her a swift look, twisted his fingers and laced them together with hers instead.

Wow. Had she imagined that fire? Or did Connor just look at her like he wanted more than hand holding?

The drive to the flower markets had been pleasant, although a little quiet. Both had buried their faces in the coffee Ava had organised. She'd brought fresh bagels after work yesterday, which she'd thrown in the toaster this morning. Smeared with cream cheese and butter, they'd been heavenly. Connor had demolished his in around four bites, so she was pretty sure he approved of her makeshift breakfast option.

Ava followed the path of least resistance, side stepping trolleys laden with roses, daisies, and baby's breath. There were fields of tulips which had the air catching in her throat, they were so striking in their perfection.

Her friend, Eliza, had said to head to the far corner away from the main entrance. That's where her stall was.

Connor stepped ahead of her, avoiding a build up around one stall. He half turned to squeeze through a gap, showing his teeth as he sent her an amused look.

His eyes shifted to her ears, and he nodded in that direction, a slight quirk forming in his brows. "What are you wearing today? Are they dice?"

She flicked her earring with her spare hand. "Sure are. Gotta roll the dice of life."

"Okay, that's pretty random, Ava. Even by your standards," he said with a chuckle.

The sound sent Ava's stomach into an oozing spin of warmth. How was this fair that her body should betray her with lascivious thoughts about her brother's best friend? She'd dated guys in the past, but nothing had turned her inside out like this. Nothing serious or that had left her permanently shattered. Perhaps because she never allowed her heart to become invested. It had taken enough knocks in this life, from a young age, that made Ava guard it pretty closely.

Connor's smile threatened that wall with one quick flash.

She needed to remember her end goal here was to secure her job and mend the rift between herself and Wyatt. How would Wyatt take it if he found out she was hanging out with Connor? Worse, what if she gave into these developing feelings and did something worse, like kiss him? Something she'd dreamed of doing last night. Over. And over. And over, again.

Heat flushed her cheeks, and she swallowed quickly, dashing a few steps ahead of Connor. Please, God, don't let him have seen her face just now.

He squeezed her hand. "That wasn't a derogatory comment." His voice came from behind her shoulder, gravelled and a few levels deeper than before.

"No, no. I know."

Somebody knock some sense into my brain, please!

"You've gone bright pink. I don't want you offended."

She yelped, tripping over an errant container, flinging water all over her feet. Droplets seeped in between her toes, shod only in a pair of thongs.

Connor steadied her body, shifting her out of the way of a trolley piled high with bunches of hydrangeas. The array of blues, violet, pinks and even a baby soft white was eye-catching.

"Ava?"

She half turned, finally looking directly at him. Searching those eyes for... something. Not even she knew what they were talking about now. She inched in a little, her heart leaping as he did the same. Her eyes flickered to his mouth, unbidden in the movement, her teeth folding the bottom corner of her lip to nibble slightly at the soft flesh.

Wishing.

Wanting.

Connor's breath whispered at her forehead. Her chin came up, her lips parting on a quick breath as the hands at her hips clenched.

"Hey, mind moving? It's our busiest day here, you love birds gotta take that business elsewhere."

Ava jumped, the tone of the man's voice registering well before his words hit home.

"Sorry!" she yelped in the man's general direction, but also to herself. "My friend's this way." She rushed her words, her feet skipping ahead, not daring to touch Connor.

She outright *refused* to contemplate what had been about to happen. Again.

* * *

"I'll also grab a few bunches of the... um... those." Connor pointed to the large daisy looking flowers. Each bunch held an array of vibrant colours: orange, deep pink, yellow. They were so happy and bright. Perfect for his mum and sisters to keep at home, and a bunch for Ava to say thank you. The yellow roses he already held in his hand were flawless, their blooms just opening. He'd do his best not to ruin them in his giant clenched fists before tomorrow. *I have the roses. Tomorrow will be fine.*

Time to ease up on that tension he had running through him, a task easier said than done when the source stood beside him, babbling and laughing with her friend.

The friend kept eyeing him, her gaze darting between him and Ava. He didn't know if he liked that assessing look. It ran far too close to his own thoughts. Like were he and Ava an item? And what the hell was with the weird energy that flashed between them, strong enough to power this whole bloody warehouse.

It was only chemistry.

If he ignored it, it would go away.

Except he was wondering if he wanted to ignore it.

Moments ago, he'd gone to kiss Ava, and no matter how he rolled that thought around in his head, it didn't elicit dread. Only happiness. He should not be feeling that way about Wyatt's sister, but facts were facts. And Connor had never been one to ignore the true black and white facts.

He wanted Ava, in a physical sense. But the more time he spent with her, he worried it went deeper than that. The way she'd spoken briefly of her mum, of how she'd been treated growing up. He couldn't relate, given his family had been nothing but a tight-knit supportive unit; however, he could clearly remember the second his dad took his last breath.

How the announcement from the doctor that remission was off the table and the cancer had come back. Every one of those moments had imploded his world, obliterating something inside him.

Ava was the first person he wanted to talk to about that. Perhaps because she didn't need him the way the rest of the women in his life did?

He shook his head, washing away those thoughts.

"They are gerberas," Ava said with a sideways smirk.

He noticed she was doing her very best to avoid meeting his gaze head on.

"Right. I'll take four bunches, and the roses. And that plant." Connor focused, blocking everyone else out. He was sure he'd have ample time to analyse these feelings tonight as he lay awake, willing his body to calm the hell down. Which was precisely what he'd done last night. And the three nights prior.

Cold showers had never been such a prominent part of his life.

"That's an indoor plant. A peace lily. They are finicky, but with love and care it will blossom." Eliza definitely flicked a look at Ava this time, her double meaning clear.

Fantastic. He was getting dating advice from a florist.

"I'll take that under advisement."

"Where are you going to put it?" Ava asked, nodding at the plant she'd taken from Eliza to hold on his behalf whilst he paid. She gripped the pot with both hands, gingerly, as though she worried just by holding it she'd do something perilous to its health.

"I… uh… not sure. Somewhere indoors."

The girls exchanged another look, and Connor could feel a slick of sweat gather at the back of his collar.

"Enjoy your flowers. Who are the roses for?" Eliza asked, handing him the other bunches and a receipt.

The sweat beaded and slid down his back just as his stomach plummeted.

"His mum," Ava inserted. "We'd better be off. I'll call you tomorrow." Ava gave Eliza a one-armed hug and started for the exit.

Connor dipped his head at Eliza and chased after Ava. "Thanks," he said, jogging to catch up and walk beside her. His arms were full of flowers, which was a little tricky to juggle. He didn't want to crush them by accident.

"No need to thank me. I could see you'd reached your limit back there. Besides, tomorrow is for you, your mum, and sisters. You're not big on sympathy. I get it."

She flashed him a quick look, and it settled the churning in his stomach. She did get it, that was part of the problem.

They walked across the carpark, avoiding the mass of cars building before his very eyes. Who knew it would be so busy here? Not that buying flowers was something he did more than twice a year. He bought them for his family's yearly trip to his father's grave, and for his mother's birthday. That was it. Always from the same florist.

He'd never thought to visit Sydney's flower markets, but it was certainly a lot cheaper. It had been nice changing up his usual routine. Without Ava's help, he'd have bought a different colour rose. The thought freaked him out. To be honest, he didn't know how that would go down with his mother, either. She was fragile enough at this time of year without him compounding the issue by not following their normal routine. He ignored the niggling voice that pointed out his mum hadn't been acting her usual way this year. He couldn't get complacent.

They reached his car, and he clicked the button to unlock it, watching Ava juggle the plant and reach for her door. "Wait a tick. I'll pop these in the boot."

"I'll nurse this one. If it tips over, your boot will be a sea of soil."

He wanted to slap his forehead. Why hadn't he thought of that?

"Plus, you drive like a rally car racer."

"What! No, I don't," he replied, indignation lacing his tone.

"Sure thing, speed racer." She hummed the theme song.

He slid past her, holding his breath as his body brushed up against her back. The fool next to him had parked too close. He only hoped Ava hadn't noticed how much his body had enjoyed that swift brush against her.

Opening her door, he stepped back, taking the plant from her outstretched hands. She threw him a quizzical look, probably because he was standing as far away as was humanely possible. Which was ridiculous. There was a car door between them. It's not as though he could jump the damn thing and pull her into his arms.

Christ. Why had he put that image in his mind?

Waiting until she was safely seated inside, and ignoring the graceful way she'd swept her legs in and the view her V-neck top afforded him, he pushed the door a little so he could step back around and deposit the plant in her lap.

Bad move. He could see right down her top, his eyes zeroing on the crevice to heaven.

He wanted to blame the summer heat, but it was still only around six. His body was on fire. Internal combustion, eat your heart out.

Ava wasn't even dressed in a way that one would call provocative. Basic tee and jeans. But it outlined every one of her subtle curves, making his fingers itch.

"Um, Connor? You can give me the plant now."

Shit. He'd been staring. He squeezed his eyes shut, then focused on her feet.

"Of course. I was waiting for you to put your safety belt on."

She wore thongs. Just your run-of-the-mill rubber thongs. *No, don't think the word thong. Or rubber. Shit!* There wasn't a thing about her that didn't make him want to strip her bare and kiss her senseless. He was losing his mind.

"Connor. It's on. Give it to me."

His heart lost the will to beat.

Did she just say…?

His eyes flung up, meeting her wide gaze head on. She was looking at him like he was stark raving mad. Heat flushed his face. With a will of iron, he wrenched his mind from the gutter and back to reality. *Remember the plant, Connor?* He could almost read those words in her eyes. Stooping down, uncaring about the damn plant, he shoved it into her waiting lap, taking care not to touch any part of her skin.

The door slamming rattled his head back into gear a little. He dragged in a few deep breaths before jogging around to the driver's seat. He would get past this. It was just chemistry. Fleeting.

He was tired and weak. And confused. There was a lot going on in his head emotionally right now. That would explain this bizarre attraction to the last girl on Earth he should want.

He'd drop her home, and that would be that. He'd thank her for her help and then not see her for the rest of the weekend.

The break would allow him to get his shit together.

Wyatt was back on Monday. That thought alone should wipe away this sexual tension.

9

"Any chance you're free for a bit of a drive?" Ava asked, biting her bottom lip.

She threw a sideways glance at Connor. He was deep in thought, his hands gripping the wheel and then stretching out. Was he muttering to himself?

"Um… Actually, I've got a thing."

Ava's heart sank. Was he trying to avoid her?

There had been an odd vibe when he'd chosen the flowers, one that had only gotten weirder once they were at the car. His looks had lasted longer, as though…

He rubbed a hand across his face and sighed. "What did you need?"

"Oh. No. The drive wasn't because I needed you to take me somewhere. I just wanted to show you a house. The one I spoke about during the meeting with Lucas yesterday."

Connor's brows rose. "A house?"

"Yes. It was a project I consulted on last year. It is only residential, obviously, since I called it a house, but it has some features I thought might interest you. To help with the project. And I'm babbling, so I'll stop now." Ava reached up and sent one of her earrings into orbit. Roll of the dice.

"Why do you like earrings so much?"

"Don't most girls?" Ava threw back flippantly.

"I guess. But I've not known one to like them as much as you. You always play with your earrings when you're nervous."

"I do? Oh." Ava pondered that, realising Connor was right. "I guess they give me a little peace. They remind me of a happier time. One of the first things my mum did after the split was take me to get my ears pierced. It was a really nice day. We ate cake for lunch afterwards because I'd cried. Then mum took me shopping and bought me like seven different pairs of earrings. I knew I couldn't wear them straight away, but, well… it was nice. We chose each pair together. It's a memory that's always stuck."

Connor didn't comment, instead he reached out and squeezed her hand. The movement warmed her heart.

"Where is the house?" he asked after a moment of silence.

"Bulli Tops. South of Sydney, past the shire, heading towards the Illawarra."

"Okay. We should drop these flowers off first or they'll die in the car."

Surprise laced her words. "Don't you have a thing?"

"It can wait."

Ava swallowed, uncertain of Connor's mood.

They took the flowers to her apartment since it was closer, before heading down the coast. They completed most of the trip in a comfortable silence.

Connor switched on music, leaving Ava to her own thoughts. The next design submission to Nexbo was due in two weeks. They had made changes, with Connor implementing some things Ava had suggested, steering clear of any that required major structural changes.

She got that.

The design he and his dad had come up with was beautiful. Aesthetically pleasing, it swirled and arched around on itself. From her suggestion, the northern side would feature self-watering vertical gardens, part of the buildings rainwater catchment. He'd amended the roof's structure to be a mosaic of solar panels, their angle controlled to shift and capture the sun.

"Why did you go into sustainability?" Connor asked, breaking into her thoughts. He tapped the steering wheel, but it wasn't really to the beat of the current pop song that was playing in the car.

"Oh. Well…" *Good question.* "I suppose I like to think about ways of makings things last. Of how to make the most of everything."

Ava glanced out the window. Dry bushland whipped past as they took a tight corner. They were getting close to the destination that she'd keyed into the car's navigation system.

Connor cleared his throat. "If you want to make the most of *everything*, why are you hiding from Wyatt the fact you're consulting for Gray's? I don't get it, Ava. You want to mend those fences, don't you?"

He shifted in his seat, his movements edgy. The tone of his voice didn't suggest anger, but it wasn't his normal easygoing cadence either.

"Because—" she bit her lower lip. Her throat constricted and a wave of emotion swamped her. Anger and sadness, and more than anything, guilt. Wyatt had every reason to hate her. She'd acted like a spoilt brat and had cost him big time "—I'm afraid," she finally whispered.

A sign ahead showed a right turn to continue to Bulli, and left to a lookout. Ignoring the monotone direction given by the car, Connor turned left. The car issued a statement to make a U-turn at the earliest convenience, as though that was always the easiest thing to do.

He stabbed a finger against the screen, shutting down the commands.

Ava stared at her hands, at the chipped clear nail polish she tried to apply every second week. It was easier to focus on her fingers than risk a look at Connor or see where he drove. She assumed the lookout.

The car pulled up short, and he cut the engine. Wind whipped at the windows, drawing Ava's attention and her gaze to the view that now lay before them.

Ava jumped at the sound of Connor's door handle clicking, the rush of air flinging her hair about her face. She scrambled to pull the straight locks back behind her ears. A moment later, her own door clicked and was pulled outwards.

She turned, her eyes hitting his bare knees. She travelled upwards, darting over muscled thighs and toned abs showcased by the light grey of his tee. Her fingers itched to reach out and feel if the fabric was as soft as it looked. He'd hooked sunglasses into the neckline. She reached his eyes. Eyes that latched on and held hers. Offering… something.

"Come on. Let's go for a walk. You can tell me why you're afraid to talk to your brother."

"I thought you didn't want to get involved?"

He scoffed, followed by a gentle roll of his eyes. "I think it's too late for that."

He reached in and unclicked her seat belt. His proximity deprived her of breath. Her heart thudded in a staccato so loud, surely he'd hear it. The movement was quick, unintentional, and yet his fingers brushed her thigh. That one touch brought her to life, her skin on guard, desperate for more. Every part of her was wired, in-tune with anything and everything that was Connor Linton. He paused as he shifted back, his head angled such that only scant centimetres separated their lips.

She bit hers, her tongue laving the spot her teeth had indented. His quick intake of breath told her the move hadn't gone unnoticed.

"You're killing me, Ava."

He locked his jaw and shifted farther away, leaving her reeling at the sense of emptiness that distance had created.

Not wanting him to see how affected she was, she jumped out of the car, wrapping her arms around her to ward off the rush of air whipping about them. The sun still glared down, so she knew it wouldn't be long until she'd be welcoming the wind, but it was a harsh variance to the still inside of the car.

By mutual agreement, they walked. The lookout was a headland and a popular one. Bikes roared as a group arrived, the throttle of their engines adding to the hectic atmosphere. A smattering of families had picnics set out, children running about, chasing hapless seagulls who were desperately seeking scraps. She turned her head and looked at the ocean, which spread in a vast expanse in a half circle before her. Left to right, all she could see was the sea.

"Are you cold?" Connor asked.

"No."

"You have goose bumps covering every inch of your body."

A shiver wracked her, and she shrugged it off. "It's just the wind, the noise."

"Why are you afraid to see your brother? What happened between you two?"

Suspicion laced his words, so she shook her head.

"It's not that. He didn't hurt me, if that's what you were thinking. Quite the opposite. I hurt him. And my dad." She dragged in air, trying to fill lungs that were threatening to stop working. "On purpose."

"*That's* why Wyatt hates you?"

"Yes. And deservedly so. I was awful."

"I'm not sure I can believe that, Ava. You seemed a little withdrawn when I last knew you. A typical teenager, maybe a bit of a loner. Certainly stubborn about letting others help you. But I never heard you say a careless word about Wyatt. You seemed to idolise him?"

She spread her hands wide, then unable to stop their movements, she wrung them together. "I wanted him to like me. I wanted him to be my family. At the same time, I was utterly jealous of everything he had. I hated him for that. I hated my dad for choosing him and not me."

Ava swallowed, blinking away the sun's glare that was too bright even though she wore sunglasses.

"I know Wyatt was trying to build up a friendship with you, when we were at school together. You always seemed to hold everyone at arm's length. Then you just disappeared from the school. Wyatt said he tried to contact you but he didn't have any luck."

Ava huffed. Just another nail drilled into her skin. Wyatt had tried to contact her as well?

"My mum couldn't afford to send me to the private school any longer. My dad, he took away his funding of my education. At least that's what she told me. I only recently found out that wasn't the case."

"What do you mean?"

"I mean my mum was lying to me. For most of my childhood, she lied. Lied about the money she received from my dad. Lied about my dad not wanting to see me. Lied about my being able to spend any time with Wyatt and my dad. She told me they didn't want to have anything to do with me. I grew up thinking I wasn't wanted, by either of them, when all the time it was my mum stopping me from being a part of their lives. And the worst part is she didn't do it because she hated me. She did it to hurt my father."

"Wow. That's. Abhorrent."

"It gets worse. You know I didn't have the best time at the private school, but when mum pulled me out, she moved us to the middle of nowhere. My schooling suffered and, honestly, the anger just built and built. I let it take over. It wasn't fair that Wyatt got the father who gave him everything, and I got zilch. I wanted to go into architecture, to get into one of the top Sydney universities. My mum had no money to spare to help me, insisting I had to take on work to help support the 'household' as she referred to it. I should have realised then that she thought very little of me. Honestly, I was just a ball of teenage anger, waiting to be set off."

"Where did you move to?"

"Out west. Past Dubbo. Honestly, it was miles away. I felt as though it had severed my dreams, they'd become useless. So I told myself I didn't care and became the typical screw-the-world teenager. I scraped through the high school certificate, my marks well off what I needed to get into any decent course. I was working more than I was attending school by that stage, anyway." Ava scuffed at the ground with her thong, clearing a little patch in the grass.

"How old were you?"

"Seventeen. I stayed with mum, and she let me because I was earning enough for both of us. I paid little attention to the fact she'd stopped working and was simply enjoying life on my meagre salary working at the local supermarket. Then soon after I turned nineteen, the wedding invitation arrived. My mother took great delight in flinging it around in my face. My anger had mellowed until that invite arrived. I'm not sure if I should be grateful that it did or horrified at the catalyst it was."

Connor looked down at her, then clasping their fingers together. He tugged on her hand, pulling them both down to sit on the grass. "Is that why you came back? Because you were angry?"

Ava tried to pull her hand away from Connor, but he held tight. Her mind shied away from the contact, but her body had other ideas, enjoying that one small connection. She swallowed, forcing the rest of her story out.

"Yes. My dad was getting married again, and the letter with the invite said he wanted to pay for me to stay with them and be a part of the wedding. All I could see was that he was throwing money around on stupid things, for me to be a sideline part of his new life, but he hadn't been able to see fit to look after my education. That just absolutely slayed me. I raged, and my mother told me I should tell my father everything I was feeling. That the only way to cleanse myself of the anger was to tell him to his face. I was such an idiot. She wanted that. She wanted me to ruin his wedding. From the day he'd ended their marriage, she'd hated him and had done everything in her power to ruin his life. Through me. I was her pawn."

Connor swore under his breath, shifting closer.

"Why didn't your father set you straight? How did you find out the truth?"

"I didn't give my dad a chance. Honestly, I strutted into that wedding, hellbent on doing everything I could to cause a scene and burn it to the ground. I upended the cake, picked up a giant piece and threw it around the room. Then I stalked to the bride and dumped a glass of red wine all over her dress and chucked a second into my father's face, screaming at him that he'd ruined my life." Ava's fingers tensed within Connor's grasp. "I can barely think of the details now without hating myself." She momentarily closed her eyes. "Wyatt picked me up and physically carried me from the room. He yelled at me, told me how ungrateful I was, how much money his dad had sunk into trying to make my life good and how I refused to so much as come over for a glass of water. He just yelled and yelled, and I stood there, furious and refusing to take in what he was saying."

Connor squeezed her hand, then broke his fingers away. The break left Ava bereft before that same hand reached out and tilted her chin towards his face. He nodded, his gaze unwavering as he shifted closer still. Connor's support threatened to break apart the fragile hold she still held on her heart.

"Wyatt's a good guy. He would have been angry at what you did to your father, sure, but when you explain I'm sure he'll understand."

"Maybe," she whispered, forcing her next words out. "Maybe if I hadn't then stolen his car and crashed it down a ravine and walked away without a second glance. At the time, I didn't even feel guilty about doing so. What type of person does that make me?"

* * *

Connor stared at the woman before him, still cupping her face gently with his palm. Tears silently tracked down her cheeks, and she tore her gaze away to stare out to sea, but not before hiding the guilt written across her face. His stomach bottomed out, his eyes following hers to stare out across the ocean but he couldn't focus.

Had Wyatt mentioned his car had been totalled back then? It wasn't news he could recall, and surely that was something he'd have remembered. Wyatt had always loved cars, the faster the better, even as a teenager. His father had bought him some type of fast sedan when he'd received his acceptance into law school. Connor had been happy for his friend, but he'd been too distracted with his own dramas to pay much heed to the news of his friends' car.

Why hadn't Wyatt mentioned it? Or had he, but Connor had been too lost to hear? Hell. It seemed none of them had come out of their teens unscathed.

He turned his head, focusing on the rapid beat at the base of her neck. "Wyatt will understand. I know he will. What I don't understand, is if you want so desperately to mend fences with him, why were you wanting to hide from him?"

"Because I didn't know how he'd react. Gray designs is my dream company to work for. This opportunity, I need it to work so I have a chance at a permanent role there."

Connor rolled this around in his mind for a while.

"Okay. It's a great company, one of the best for sure, but isn't mending fences with Wyatt just as important?"

"Gray Designs is *all* about family. That's one thing I've never had, not really. Everything they stand for speaks to something inside me. I want to be a part of that. I can't explain it any better than that. You know me. I want my cake and to eat it too. I want the job with Gray Designs, I want to become a part of that family, but I equally want to mend my relationship with Wyatt and my dad. I worried if I tried to do both at once it would all fall apart."

Connor nodded. Somehow that made a weird sort of sense. If Ava had written off her brother's car in a fit of rage, even over ten years previously, he was sure there would be some fireworks to rustle through before they'd be able to make peace.

"I'm ashamed of how I acted. It didn't matter that I didn't have all the facts. What I did? That behaviour isn't excusable. I'm not sure Wyatt will forgive me. I'm not sure *I* would forgive me."

"Has your father?"

"I don't know." She shrugged. "I reached out to him two weeks ago. I got a message back yesterday, but then we had the rose drama. We're going to meet for coffee early next week. I need to apologise and explain. He seems to want to hear from me."

"It sounds like he's ready to forgive you. And I'm sure once he knows the full details…"

Ava scrunched her nose, then let out a sigh. "Apparently he knows what my mum did. That's how I found out. I found a half-written letter to my father, from my mum, in an old stack of papers. According to my father, she loved nothing more than to taunt him with all the ways she was holding me hostage from his life—her added little knife twist. When I confirmed coffee with him last night, he told me he knew what my mother had been doing all those years. But, apparently, with their agreement, he couldn't approach me directly. My mother was smarter than she looked in some ways." Her lips pulled into a flat line. "And meaner."

Connor could scarcely believe anyone could be that cruel. To use their children in such a horrid way. No wonder Ava had always looked angry and unapproachable at school. Something about her had always drawn him to her. He'd wanted to help her. Maybe she was right, and maybe he had a hero complex. Ava brought that out in him now; he wanted to scoop her up in his arms and make her pain disappear.

"If your mum had been taunting him, why didn't he tell you once you once you turned eighteen? Did you ever confront your mum?"

"He'd hoped the wedding would be the time he could tell me everything and explain, but I didn't give him the chance, and then I disappeared. I would've loved the opportunity to confront my mother, but after I got back from the wedding, she'd packed up and left. No note, nothing, so I didn't bother to try to find her. Some things Wyatt yelled at me… they gave me the kick I needed. I couldn't just disregard them. I was tired of feeling angry and working in a job I hated. So I worked and saved, studied at night to do all the bridging courses required to get into architecture. I got accepted into a course in Western Australia and rebuilt my life." She drew her knees up to her chest, hugging them. "It wasn't what I'd dreamed, but I worked hard. I studied a master's in sustainability, built up friendships, established a good work ethic. When Nexbo reached out, I knew it was time to follow my original dreams." She stalled, dragging in a deep breath. "Then I found the letter, and here I am."

Connor looped his arms around Ava, pulling her in close. She cried, each quiet sob a pin prick to his heart. He held her until the tears came to an end, knowing the only thing he could offer her was his support.

* * *

Ava had no words left, she was exhausted, but telling Connor had lifted a weight. It shouldn't feel this good to have told him. Her story needed to go to Wyatt and her father, yet having Connor sit beside her, having him look at her as though he got it, his arms around her, holding her like she was something precious, shifted her heart in a way it hadn't felt for a long time.

She didn't know what that meant for them, but she knew their relationship had changed. They weren't just work colleagues. She wanted Connor and wasn't afraid to admit that. Her attraction to him was undeniable. And sharing her turmoil with him now had broken another barrier.

"Come to dinner tonight. With my family."

Her eyes flung towards him. "I don't want to intrude. I know it's a big weekend for you."

"I make burritos every year, the night before we go to Dad's grave. It might be nice to have someone else there instead of just being our morose selves. I know it's not the family you wanted, or deserved, but I'd like you there with me."

How did she say no to that? Connor had just heard her sad story and was still talking to her. He hadn't walked off or told her what a horrid person she was. If he wanted her there, then there she'd be.

Connor walked through the door, noticing Ava hesitated on the threshold. He threw a reassuring smile over his shoulder.

They'd spent a bit of time just sitting on the headland after Ava's confession. It was a revelation, and Connor now understood why Ava was putting off her confrontation with Wyatt. It also put into perspective how out of touch Connor had been with his best friend during a tough time for both of them. He still didn't know how he'd not known Ava had stolen her brother's car. Surely Wyatt would have mentioned that?

After a while, Ava had rallied, saying they really should go see the house. It had been worth the trip. Not just hearing Ava's story—that had been a lot—but the house gave Connor a physical view on some concepts Ava had been talking about for his design. He still didn't know how much more he wanted to change, but he could better understand Ava's ideas.

Walking into the lounge room, it surprised him to find his mum and both sisters lounging on the couch. They all held a glass of champagne.

A giant bunch of red roses took centre stage on the coffee table.

"Connor!" his mum yelped, jumping up. Heat loomed in her cheeks and if Connor didn't know better, he'd say she looked guilty.

He walked across the room and kissed her cheek. "Mum, this is Ava. Wyatt's sister. Ava, this is my mum, Carly. On the couch are Cassie and Clare." He pointed to each of his sisters.

Cassie offered a giant grin, her eyes darting between him and Ava.

He gave her a warning look, which only resulted in her grin growing wider.

"I've invited Ava for dinner. Sorry, I'll get it started now."

He went to walk to the kitchen, but his mum reached out a hand, her fingers cold against his arm. Probably from her champagne glass.

He frowned at that. It looked as though they were celebrating. A chill spread up his arm.

"Darling, we've ordered Thai for dinner. We thought it might be nice to try something else."

Connor glanced at Clare and Cassie, both who'd lost their smiles and now wore similar expressions of anxiety. He looked to his mum, her eyes wide but set.

Unease sat like lead in the pit of his gut. "Okay. You don't want dad's burritos?"

"Well, my doctor suggested I try to change up the process a bit this year."

"You said you cancelled your doctor's appointment."

"I did. I'm going to someone new."

"A new doctor?"

"Yes, dear."

"Okay." He was nodding like one of those bobbing heads that sit on a car dashboard. He forced his body to stop. "I found yellow roses," he added lamely. Looking at the red roses, more tingles shot up his arm as his gaze shifted to the yellow ones. They appeared kind of dull and sad in comparison.

"The thing is, we thought we might change that too." Clare spoke this time. She shifted to the edge of the lounge, offering a tentative smile.

"Am I missing something here? You're all looking at me like I'm about to have a mental breakdown." Connor shrugged, though he didn't know what at.

"We weren't sure how you'd respond, to the changes."

He wanted to say he didn't care. The changes didn't bother him. A numbness entered his mind. The sort that he used to feel back when his dad had first been diagnosed, and every time he'd return from the doctor. In limbo. That's how he'd best describe it. A disconnect between his mind and body. An inability to process what was going on.

He needed time.

And space.

"Sure. You should change things. I'll go throw these out."

Before anyone could respond, he marched out of the room, the numbness spreading to every inch of his body. The minute he stepped through that threshold into the corridor beyond the living room, he realised he'd abandoned Ava.

Did he go back? His weight shifted between his feet, neither taking him forwards or backwards. His mind screamed at him to go back. It was rude to have left her like that, and yet he desperately needed space.

A jittery energy coursed through him, his thoughts darting in a million different directions but not one he could pin down. One look at the roses in his hand zeroed his focus on that one thing. He shifted away from the lounge room, walking out the laundry, pushing through the back door and into the fresh air. He marched straight to the compost bin, stalling again at that point.

Could roses go in the compost?

Could he just throw these out?

He brushed the petals against his palm; the colour soothed him.

"Connor?"

He turned in his mother's direction, and she took tentative steps towards him. Words formed on his lips, but he couldn't push them past.

"You're upset with us." She reached him, placing a hand out on his arm, rubbing it in a circular motion. Just like she'd always done when he was younger.

"No," he retorted, surprised at the bite in his tone.

She smiled. "You are, and that's okay. We sprang a few changes on you. I know change isn't something you like. But this needs to happen, we need to rip the Band-Aid off."

"I'm not sure I follow."

"Darling, we've been doing this same thing for years. At first it made sense, it helped all of us cope. But last year, after my minor episode, I knew enough was enough. I couldn't live with the looks you kept giving me afterwards, as though I was going to leave you too. I went to see a counsellor, to talk through all the things I've never dealt with. They've been amazing and have really helped me see I was stuck in this same rotation. I've been trying to tell you this past month, but you've had me under a microscope and haven't listened."

"I—" he stopped. Hadn't his mum been acting differently? Wasn't this what he wanted? For her to not be so fragile? Why hadn't he seen that for what it was, instead of panicking that she wasn't falling apart?

"I spoke to your sisters, and they agree it's time to change how we deal with this anniversary. We don't want to be sad anymore, we want to celebrate the memory of your father. Everything you've done for us has held us together, but it's time to let that go. You can't keep trying to hold everyone else up. You're not living your life, and I feel responsible for that. You've become so afraid of change you don't even see it for what it is now. A good thing."

Her hand still rubbed his arm, one aspect he could cling too. Was he afraid of change? Her words rattled something inside him, but he didn't think he'd go as far as saying that. They could do things differently. He didn't have to cook burritos the evening before they visited the grave. They didn't have to take yellow roses if his mum didn't want to.

Something inside him rolled over, his stomach in knots at the thought of not having those actions to tick off his list. But that was okay, he would just change them to the new actions. If they wanted to order Thai instead, he would put that in his diary. They could order different coloured flowers or even different types each year. That certainly made life easier. If they wanted to drink champagne and talk about their father and celebrate his life, then that is what they'd do.

"Okay." He nodded, pursed his lips, and mentally added tasks to his list.

"Whilst we're on the topic, I need to tell you I've got myself a job."

Connor's mind blanked. "Sorry, what?"

"I have a job. Nothing glamorous, just at the local medical centre working at reception. I've been brushing up on my skills and took a medical administration course. That's why I went out Thursday, for the interview. I didn't want to tell anyone in case I didn't get it. I'd be too embarrassed."

Connor felt like a heel. He'd been thinking she was having a mental breakdown when really she was just pulling her life together. "Oh, mum, I'm such an idiot." He pulled her into a hug. How long had it been since he'd really listened to his mum, instead of just seeing what he expected to see?

"I'm proud of you," he spoke into the top of her head, which barely reached his chin.

"I'm proud of me too. It's taken longer than it should, but it's time for me to get out of this life rut. It's time for you to stop being my full-time carer and go live your life, the one that involves you being a young man who is carefree and not tied to ensuring everything in mine and your sister's lives are on track."

"I'm carefree. I don't feel tied down."

"Maybe not. Maybe you don't feel that now because it's been going on so long, but you are. I think it's become second nature that you don't even see it."

He didn't really know what to say to that, so instead he pulled her back in for another hug. The screen door at the laundry squeaked behind them, and a quick glance over his shoulder showed Ava walking towards them. She was hugging her middle, her eyes hooded.

"I'm going to leave you two youngsters to chat." His mum gave him one last squeeze and then she walked to the laundry, giving Ava a quick hug on the way.

The smile that lit Ava's face with that one small move created a hiccup in his chest.

She reached his side. "Why don't you put the roses in a vase. They are too beautiful to be thrown in the compost." Her hand reached out, offering to take them.

She was right, they shouldn't be wasted. "Sure."

Leading the way towards his studio, he fished the keys out of his pocket, then unlocked the door and pushed it open. The sky beyond was deepening to a warmer blue, a tinge of red seeping into the fluffs of white that dotted low on the horizon. It was later in the day than he'd realised. But then, that shouldn't surprise him. They hadn't left Bulli until after three thirty.

The day seemed endless. But in a good way.

It had certainly been a lot.

Ava stepped past, her shoulder brushing his chest as she did. His frame was half blocking the doorway.

"This is nice."

He looked around the room, seeing it properly for what felt like the first time. It was stark, devoid of colour. "It's bland."

She threw him a grin over her shoulder. "Nothing a lick of paint wouldn't fix. Where shall I put these? Do you have a vase?"

"Good question. I'll look in the kitchen." After a quick search, he produced a water jug that he'd been using to store cold water in his fridge.

Ava arranged them on the small coffee table that sat before his over-sized leather couch. His giant TV dominated the room, which he really only used to watch action flicks and catch the news in the mornings.

"Thank you, for coming with me today. I'm sorry I intruded on a bit of a moment just now." She reached out a hand, placing it against his forearm. "Are you okay?"

Connor rubbed at his jaw. He still wasn't sure he could answer that with any certainty. His mother's words that he was afraid of change didn't ring true. Sure, he was a little shocked, but he was fine with the changes she and his sisters wanted. He didn't mind she was returning to work, the type of flowers… Any of it. He was fine. What was unsettling him was that no one consulted him first, as though they thought he couldn't handle it. He didn't enjoy being the last to know.

That hurt.

Their not believing in him enough to talk to him first, that they decided to just make the changes and show him the results after the fact, that was what sent him spinning off axis. His world felt off key, his feet now on the ceiling or something equally ridiculous. He was a loose screw holding too many things above his head.

He looked about his space, and all he felt was on edge. He'd spent years living here, and yet with one afternoon it had ceased to feel like home. Now it just felt cold.

The one bright spot in the space stood before him. Ava. With her fresh-faced beauty, casual smile and ridiculous earrings. Dice. Who wore dice at their ears?

What had she said… you have to roll the dice to see where life takes you? Or something equally bonkers that was being passed off as profound.

Had he rolled his dice? Was this what he wanted for his life right now? His mum had implied he'd stopped living, but he didn't entirely agree with that either. He was living the life he wanted. He had a job he loved, great friends, and well… His gaze zeroed in on Ava.

"What?" She quirked a brow, her grin turning a little goofy as he studied every inch of her face.

He walked across to where she stood, crowding her personal space.

"I'm tired of this, Ava. I'm tired of pretending." He looked at her, *really* looked. No shying away, no holding back. His eyes gleamed at what he saw: deep blue orbs that became almost black as lust swept across her depths.

She met his gaze for one beat, then another before she said, "to hell with this." Grabbing his head, she pulled him down, closing the gap between them. Her lips met his, her palms lightly caressing his cheeks.

His world tilted again—the right way up. How had he held off? Kissing Ava was like the first breath dragged into his lungs after a punishing run. It was the first sip of cold beer after a hard day's work; it was punchy and organic. She bit his bottom lip, dragging at it until it flicked back against his teeth.

This wasn't enough.

Her lips against his weren't enough. Would they ever be enough?

He wanted more.

Needed more.

He cupped his hands over hers, his heartbeat ravaging within his chest, thudding to its own heated beat. He changed the angle of the kiss, taking it deeper, their tongues twisting and tangling with the other, searching for that perfect link. She moaned, which turned to a groan as she broke away.

"Um, we have to stop."

"Why?" he panted, then realised that was not an okay thing to say. "Shit. Sorry, of course. If you don't want to." Stepping back, he plonked his hands on his lips as he puffed air in and out, desperately trying to level out his breathing and other parts of his body. He didn't need to look down to know he was sporting an impressive tent in his shorts. He didn't want to stop. Kissing Ava had tasted better than Christmas, Easter, and his birthday all rolled into one, but if she wasn't on the same page, then he would respect her wishes. Even if his body was physically aching to close the gap between them once more. He might actually spontaneously combust if she walked out right now.

"No! I don't want to stop. I mean—" She slapped a palm to her face, scoffing. "Give me a minute to find my brain, which has turned to mush, much like the rest of me I might add. Honestly, Connor, kissing you needs to come with a warning."

Heat spread through his torso at her words. "So you liked it then?" A slow grin spread across his face, noticing how flustered she was and enjoying seeing the heat in those expressive eyes.

"Yes!" She speared him with a heated look which turned into an eye-roll. "But that's not the issue. I told your sisters we'd join them for dinner. The Thai food is probably already here, which means we're probably going to get a visitor real soon."

The mention of his sisters was like being doused with water. Cold water. Filled with ice.

"Oh. Yes, that puts a dampener on, um… this." He circled a finger between them.

Her eyes slipped down to his chest, and then lower. Her cheeks bloomed brighter than before.

"Behave," he murmured, though he wasn't sure if the word was for Ava or his dick that was refusing to heed the call of the imminent interruption.

Her lips twitched. "Should I go tell your sisters that we're going to go out, or something? Instead. If you want to?"

God, she was cute when flustered. "I don't want to go out. But I'm not sure I want to stay here either." He dragged in air; her delicious scent still filled his nostrils. He regretted his next words before he spoke them. "Maybe we need to rain check until I can find us a suitable place where we'll be alone. Truly alone. Minus the threat of my nosy sisters or newly energised mother."

Her bark of laughter was short, followed by her shaking her head. "Yeah, I'm definitely past the age where I could handle a mum or sister walking in on us."

She stepped closer, her fingers tangled with his. Her head tilted, and she brushed her nose against his. The move cracked his chest open, threatening his composure where she was concerned.

"I might know somewhere," she whispered, her eyes finding and capturing his.

He swallowed, desperately willing his body to calm the excitement those four words had evoked.

"Somewhere close?"

She grimaced. "Do you call Alexandria close?"

"No. But are you sure you're happy for me to come back to your place?"

"Wild horses couldn't stop me dragging you back there right now. I want you, Connor. Kind of badly." She grinned, stepping in closer still and running her other hand along the side of his thigh.

Her movements were going to kill him if she kept that up.

A knock sounded against his front door.

He groaned. "Go away," he shouted, not caring which of his sisters it was. He knew it wouldn't be his mum again. She'd want him to have his space after their chat.

"Thai's here," Cassie's voice came through the door. "Or shall I say you're otherwise… engaged?" she giggled.

"Tell mum we'll take a rain check. Ava and I are going out."

"Enjoy yourselves," came the reply.

His eyes hadn't left Ava's the whole time. "We will."

va thought she'd feel nervous on the drive back to her apartment. They'd stopped there briefly before heading to his mother's house in North Sydney. She'd have brightly coloured gerbera's awaiting her arrival.

They'd covered a lot of kms today and she was ready to be out of the car. Permanently. And not just because then she'd be able to do what she'd been dreaming of all this past week—stripping Connor naked and stepping into his arms.

The thought sent heat straight to her core.

"You're quiet," Connor murmured.

"Just thinking."

"Care to share?"

"I'm thinking about how I'm going to strip you bare, drop to my knees, and take you into my mouth."

The car swerved a little. "Shit, Ava."

She giggled, enjoying throwing him off balance. "What? You asked."

Part of her wanted to reach over and rub this thigh, a brief prelude to what they both wanted, but she also wasn't crazy. They were still a few minutes from her apartment, and Sydney traffic on a Saturday evening was never forgiving.

Sydney traffic, anytime, sucked, to be honest.

He pulled into the underground parking, Ava directing him to the space that was allocated to her apartment. The park was small and tight to get into, but Connor didn't seem phased. The engine shut off and silence took over. Ava unclipped her seat belt, noting that Connor hadn't.

"Now who's quiet."

"I care about you, Ava. I don't know where this is going, but I wanted you to know that. This isn't just a reaction to earlier… I've wanted you almost from the moment I spotted you again in the foyer."

She jolted, surprised by his words and serious tone. She'd expected Connor to be flirty and continue the lightness they'd had going.

"I care about you too. I know this complicates matters, and complication isn't really your thing."

"No. Well, at least it wasn't before you strolled into my life. I can't say I mind though."

Ava opened her mouth to say something about Wyatt and snapped it shut. Kissing Connor had complicated her work life and her plans to mend fences with Wyatt. Having sex with Connor would blast 'complicated' right out of the water. Yet even knowing this could only end with tears, possibly hers, didn't make her want to stop.

It didn't appear to be giving Connor any pause either, so why bring it up?

The walk up to her apartment was leisurely. She clasped his hand in hers, their fingers entwined. When she took hers away to search for her key card, he captured it back swiftly once they were through the main door into the complex.

Had she cleaned her apartment recently? *Who cares.*

Pushing her door inwards, she yanked Connor in after her. Tossing her bag on the ground, she used her free hand to bring his mouth down on hers, his body slamming the door shut behind them as she leaned her full weight into his.

His lips broke from hers briefly. "Slow down. We have all night."

"I don't want slow." She kissed him again, tension building in her body. "I want now."

He chuckled. "Far from it for me to stand in your way. I can see you like getting what you want."

Ava didn't care for words, she cared about action. Her body ached to feel Connor against her, to explore every delectable inch of the torture that had been facing her this past week.

Had it only been a week?

Thinking of how little time she'd known this Connor and how invested she was sent her stomach into a flutter and her mind into lockdown.

Time to wipe all thoughts and only feel.

Stepping back, she whipped her T-shirt over her head, enjoying the dark hunger in Connor's eyes.

"You are a threat to my health." His eyes worshipped her chest. Her bra was firmly fastened, though his gaze burned through the lace, heating her skin instantly.

He ran a single finger down her chest, starting from the apex of her collarbone, down to her navel. She squirmed when he reached that little indent of her belly.

"Ticklish?" His brow quirked, an evil gleam lighting those sky-blue eyes.

"No," she stated, adamantly. Too adamantly, perhaps. Her head shook, her mouth forming another O before he pounced.

His fingers tortured her rib cage, darting in at the sides. Gentle, yet enough to drive her insane with the soft touch. Her laughter echoed in the small space, his whispered words at her ear. "Sure you aren't ticklish?"

"No!"

"Surrender."

"Never!"

His words caressed her skin, and though she was squirming and giggling, the tension building inside her was different. Her heart leapt as he grabbed her around her waist and swung her up into his arms.

She rested her hands behind his neck. "Now what do you plan to do," she asked, still panting from their exertions during the tickling match.

"This." He leaned in and hovered his lips scant millimetres from hers, a wispy-soft peck at the corner of one side of her mouth, followed by the other. He placed butterfly kisses along her jawline.

The change in tempo threw her. The atmosphere had changed, entering a depth that Ava didn't know how to decipher.

He sat down on her couch, keeping her body tucked up close against his chest. Her legs stretched out against the soft cotton weave of the fabric. Years of use had stripped it of any roughness.

She shifted, bringing their mouths together, fusing her lips to his as she moaned. Pinpricks spread along her arms, the cool air mingling with the intensity of his body heat. And anticipation. The room glowed with it. Shifting again, unable to still her movements, she broke away for only a moment to bring her legs to either side of his thighs, straddling him. She gasped as her core met his rock hard bulge. She dove at his mouth, kissing him with passion and fire, nipping at the plump skin of his bottom lip.

His mouth moved from hers, kissing a line down the side of her neck, leading a trail of fire with each touch of his lips against her bare skin. She writhed, desperate to speed him up but also longing for this feeling to continue forever.

Her body was a furnace of need, wanting him to set her free.

It wasn't just Connor's body she wanted; the realisation giving her pause. It was the man beneath that. The passion he'd shown for his work all week, the memory of his father that he desperately wanted to showcase through his design. That spoke to Ava on a level she'd never experienced with a man before. He'd had the perfect family dynamic ripped swiftly from him. She'd had no family dynamic and had always wanted it. They should be total opposites, and yet they weren't.

Connor was a good guy. The sort she'd always craved to have in her life but had never really found.

"Or never let in," her mind whispered.

Was that the case? Had she never really let anyone in before?

"You've gone quiet," Connor said against the skin at her right shoulder. He drew a soft pattern with his nose. "Do you want to stop?"

That question snapped her focus directly back to him. "No. I don't want to stop. I was just thinking we haven't really known each other long. It's odd. I'm not usually like this with a guy."

"I'm not usually like this with a guy either."

She rolled her eyes at Connor's smirk. "You really aren't funny."

"So people keep telling me. Seriously, though. This is… different, for me too. You aren't alone there. I feel a weird connection to you; I guess I always have. Back when we were at school together, I was always more concerned about you than I probably should have been. You were so angry all the time, yet I sensed beneath that there was something driving you. I admired your strength. You didn't deserve the hand life dealt you."

His words spread warmth from her fingers to her toes, some of the ice around her heart melting away.

"Thank you." Her fingers laced with his, her eyes captured in the heat and something else that simmered in his gaze. A section of her shied away from that look, scared at what was being offered.

She squeezed his hand then broke away, running the tips of her fingers against the stretch of bare skin where his shirt had bunched up. Lifting the hem, she gave it a few tugs before Connor sat forward, giving her unfettered access to stripping that fabric barrier away, leaving nothing but an expanse of muscled skin and perfection for her to feast her eyes on. How many hours did one have to put in at the gym to maintain a six-pack like that?

"I run," he answered. The unspoken question that must have shown in her eyes.

"I run occasionally, too, but I'm not rocking Thor-like abs."

"Nope. You're rocking something much better."

Gripping her hips, he lifted her as though she weighed nothing, bringing her up to her knees. Her tummy fluttered at the move, at the careful way he held her, as though she was precious and meant something to him.

His head bent, kissing across her belly, across her navel and to one hip. She thrust forward, drawn to the delicious feeling of his fiery mouth against her flesh. He kissed a line along the top of her jeans, his breath stopping at her top button.

She yanked at the jeans, his fingers nudging hers away as he undid the button with ease. Tugging at the zipper until it stopped, he then slid the denim down her hips, taking her lace undies along with them. She stood to remove the jeans, doing a hop and shimmy to get the darned things off. Why did she choose skin-tight jeans today?

He chuckled, probably enjoying the show of her jumping about, practically naked, her breasts barely contained in the lace cups as she jiggled and fought with her pants

"Who the hell invented tight jeans. There is no way to make stripping these off sexy."

"On the contrary, from where I'm sitting, the view is one of the best."

Ava freed one ankle, closely followed by the other. She kicked the offending piece of clothing away before straddling Connor once more. "You're overdressed."

His only response was to continue kissing. The mixture of soft wet mouth and heat so close to her core had her writhing with need. He ran a finger along the top of her thigh, then dipped across to slip a finger inside her. She cried out, rubbing against him, needing more.

"You're so wet."

A moan ripped from her throat as his finger deserted her. *Come back!* She thrust her hips forward, her body moving on autopilot, seeking, searching, needing to feel him inside her and lay waste to this heaviness that was building within. She couldn't think, desperate only to feel his touch against her once more.

His arm came around her, running his fingertips up her spine, curling her into him like a cat. His mouth sucked on her bare skin, the attention sending fresh waves of need to her breasts and beyond. With a gentle flick, her bra came undone, the lace rubbing gently against her pebbled nipples, which were heavy with need. Her entire body craved Connor.

She slid the straps down, whipping the bra off and sending it flying before she ran her fingers through his hair. Tugging on the tips, she tilted his head back, taking his mouth with hers once more. She couldn't stop moving, her body filled with an energy that desperately craved release.

His mouth broke from hers. "God, you're beautiful. I want to taste every part of you."

True to his word, he took one peak into his mouth, sucking and laving at the fullness until she cried out. The attention brought her so close to the brink she wondered if he'd bring her undone just by kissing her breasts. She anguished when he moved his attention to her other one—her need for him overriding all else.

"Now. Connor. Condom." She panted, the words barely legible for her ears.

But he had other plans. He spun her to the couch, laying her down. The cool air against the tips of her nipples had her sucking in a breath. The contrast to Connor shifting and breathing on her hips, then shuffling lower had her tensing with desire. She wanted to pull him up on top of her, to feel him inside her, but the devilish pleasure in his eyes as he flicked her a quick glance stilled any thought to movement. He parted her, dragging his tongue up the full length of her.

She cried out, but she didn't care. Couldn't care. She was nothing but the pleasure Connor was giving, his tongue twisting and licking and diving inside her. Need built, rushing through her. An intense heaviness and warmth. Her hips thrust of her own will, bringing her closer, closer… Until she came apart. She screamed Connor's name; the word leaving her lips unbidden. Every inch of her tingled, feeling soft cotton beneath her and spiky bristles of his jaw against her thigh as he continued to kiss her. She was alive with feeling and yet too lethargic after her release to form any coherent thought or sentence.

Her pants slowly invaded the fogginess as she materialised from the aftereffects.

"Wow," she said, breathing out.

"Good wow, I hope?" Connor raised a cocky brow, knowing full well it was good.

He grinned at her, and she knew she'd never be able to look at his mouth again without feeling desire. Her orgasm had been intense, rocketing through every scant inch of her.

"Yes. Good. I'm sure we can do better though?"

His brow dropped, his eyes narrowing, alight with a mischievous glint. "Challenge accepted."

Rolling away, he stood, freeing himself from his gym shorts, his cock bursting free. Ava couldn't help the gasp that left her lips. Desire seeped back in, heat already building in her core just from the sight of Connor before her, stark naked.

He offered his hand to hers, which she grabbed, pulling her to a standing position with one quick tug. Stepping into his arms, she went to her tippy toes to kiss him, needing that connection. They were joined from chest to thigh. His hard length throbbed against her tummy.

She broke away. "Please tell me you—"

He kissed her once, cutting off her words. Bending down, he grabbed a foil packed from his wallet and held the shiny square up in triumph.

Ava snatched it from him, her eyes twinkling.

She slapped a palm to his chest and pushed, sending him tumbling back onto the couch. She followed, straddling his naked form as she ripped open the foil. Removing the condom, she rolled it onto his hard length. Connor groaned as she did, the sound addictive. She gripped him, pumping her hand slowly upwards, each movement bringing him pleasure.

"Unless you want this over right now, I suggest you stop that," he panted, each word heaved from his lips.

"Spoil sport." Her grin widened, and with one last tug, she shifted, positioning him at her entrance before sliding down and bringing him inside her at the same time he tilted his hips. He filled her to the hilt, the one slow move drawing moans from both of them.

"Fuck." The word dragged from Connor's lips. "You feel… Heaven."

Ava shifted, tilting her hips around to grind herself on his length. She arched her back, her bare breasts scraping the sparse hair of Connor's chest. He gripped her hips, slowing her movements, his breathing hard.

He took her right nipple in his mouth, sucking, the move feeling like payback. She writhed again, her body once more not her own. She hadn't thought she'd feel this way so soon, thinking she'd bring Connor undone as he had her, but her body had other ideas. Pressure and heat forged its way back almost the instant she'd taken him inside her. His length filled her, and the more she shifted, the more intensity she felt, her body locking up, ready to explode.

His teeth scraped against her peak, and she mewled at the immeasurable pleasure that one nip sent spiralling through her. Needing more, and uncaring that she was being demanding, she shifted, her shoulders arching back to bring her other nipple to his mouth. Everything about her wanted more. Demanding more.

She ground against him, locking her muscles in to squeeze him inside her, the move dragging her name from his lips. The mood switched. He clutched her hips, grinding upwards as his hands guided her in circles. Their movements edgy, erratic. Desperate for release.

Connor cried out, the sound sending her into her own spiral of ecstasy. He continued to pump into her, her body falling to his, breathing in his heat, warmth and scent that filled her mind, body and soul. She was drained, completely sapped of energy, and wrung bare. Making love had never been this passionate, or intense with anyone before.

Never had she felt such compatibility and complete release to be herself.

She snuggled against his chest, her heart flipping over as his arms came around her back, pulling her in closer to him.

As though he never wanted to let her go.

During the night, they'd shifted from the couch to Ava's bedroom. The bed filled most of the room, and Connor had joked it was bigger than his. She'd winked and dragged him in, stating it hadn't been christened with any amazing sex yet. What could a guy do with such a request? He couldn't let the lady down.

He'd surfaced in the early hours, enjoying the miniscule amount of light that was seeping into the horizon. A snippet of it laid across Ava's slumbering face. In sleep she was so peaceful, so still. Compared to the vibrant energy and expressiveness he saw on her face each day, it was quite the contrast.

She stirred, rolling on her side and snuggling closer to him. He propped his head on his hand, using a finger to drag a few strands of auburn hair that had slid across her face.

A sigh slipped out, the whispers of a smile hinting at the corner of her mouth.

"Morning," she mumbled, her eyes still firmly shut.

"Morning." He leaned in and kissed her nose. "I should probably get going."

Her eyes jumped open. Their clear blue depths met his. "Is it morning already?"

"Early morning. The sun's just thinking of getting up."

"Well then, maybe you should think about letting it do that first." A grin slid across her face, her eyes deepening in a way that told him she had a hidden agenda to keep them in bed.

Not that he minded.

But he needed to get home.

"I can't. Today…" he let the word drift.

Ava scrunched her eyes tight. "Sorry, of course. I'm such a klutz. Of course you need to get going."

Her eyes opened with a level of concern that steadied a little of the turmoil inside him. He wanted to stay in bed with her. All day. And not just to continue his exploration of every inch of her glorious body. But because being with her soothed something inside him he hadn't realised he'd even been battling. Being confronted by his mother yesterday had thrown him. Not because of her newfound courage and strength, he'd loved being witness to that, but because it had brought to light his own failing.

She'd accused him of fearing change. Except he didn't feel that.

Change was fine.

"Connor?" Ava's question brought him back to the present. Her brows quirked, a soft indent forming there that he reached out and soothed away.

"I'm fine."

"Are you sure? Just now, you looked… sad."

"Just a lot going on."

"Understandably. This doesn't have to be anything. You know. You and me. It can just remain as last night or whatever."

"Or whatever?" He raised a brow. "How coherent. Is that what you'd prefer? To keep last night as just a once off."

Connor tried to still the rapid beating that had taken over inside his chest. He hadn't realised Ava would consider last night to just be a casual hook up. It had felt… more. So much more.

She bit her lip, sliding the bottom piece out from underneath. It turned deep rouge from the move. His body stirred, wanting to lean forward and kiss the plump flesh, but he didn't dare.

"No. I don't want last night to be a once off. But I don't want to add anything to what's already on your plate. We can just keep this casual and fun. Whenever it suits."

"I'm not sure that we could do this whenever it suits. Something tells me that taking a week off probably wouldn't go down well at work right now. Because that's what suits me, keeping you in bed for at least a week."

Heat spread high across her cheeks. "Now there's an offer I'd struggle to turn down. But I guess you're right. Work would probably want to know why we both disappeared."

"I'm probably not meant to be sleeping with the enemy right now, anyway."

"Hey! I'm not the enemy." She stuck her tongue out at him, and he used her distraction to drag her closer, kissing her. She fit perfectly within his arms.

"I thought you needed to go," she murmured, sliding a leg up along his. His body was fully awake now, exploring her naked form.

"Maybe we have a few minutes," he whispered at her ear. "More than a few minutes." Then he took both of them into blissful exploration and oblivion.

Much later, satiated and dozing, Connor looked at his watch and groaned. "I do need to think about moving soon. We usually go around ten or eleven. Before lunch."

He didn't know if his mum and sisters wanted to change that as well, but he should at least be home so they could discuss. It was just after eight, so he had time.

"Do you want coffee? Breakfast?"

Ava slid from the bed, her naked body padding over to the door and grabbing a slinky gown from the back. She slid it on, giving Connor a pang of disappointment, which was short-lived. The fabric clung to her every curve, highlighting her breasts, which were still pebbled from his most recent attentions. Something about Ava was bringing him to life. Not that he didn't normally enjoy sex, but he didn't feel the least bit satiated after being with her. He wanted her again, even now, so soon after having her come apart in his arms. She made him feel like a horny teenager. Not that he'd ever really explored that part of his life to the full.

That thought arrested him.

"I keep losing you this morning." She offered a soft smile, though he could sense the question behind her words.

"Coffee would be great."

He hopped out of bed, pulling up the bedclothes and smoothing them into place. He tucked the sheet in and plopped the pile of pillows back on top.

"You're very domesticated." Ava eyed his handiwork.

He walked past, blatantly naked, enjoying that her gaze had shifted from the bed to his chest and beyond.

He dropped a quick kiss against her forehead. "I had to be." Collecting his T-shirt and shorts from the lounge room where they lay strewn amongst Ava's clothes, he then pulled them on and picked up her things, folding them on to a chair.

"Do you want to talk about it?"

"You know much of it. My mum ceased functioning after we lost dad. There wasn't anyone else to keep the household from turning into a pigsty, and I suppose I enjoyed having things to do. I... couldn't stop. If I stopped, I worried I'd—"

"Not get going again?"

"I guess so. Yes. Anyway. Being domesticated isn't exactly a bad thing."

"I'm not complaining." Ava went to the small kitchenette that was part of the open plan lounge area. She hit a few buttons on a fancy-looking coffee machine, whirring it to life.

Connor cleared his throat. "My mum, yesterday, said I was afraid of change." He pulled himself up onto one of the bar stools, enjoying Ava pottering about in her domain.

She flicked him a glance. "Do you think you're afraid of change?"

"No."

The machine beeped, and she placed two cups on the tray, hitting another button to disperse a deep black liquid. The scent of strong coffee filled the air, and he drank it in.

Ava removed the cups from the machine, not asking him how he preferred his favourite morning pick-me-up, but he noted she added a teaspoon of sugar, serving it black. Her observation of how he liked his coffee gave him a little more insight to her, bringing a smile to the corner of his mouth.

She skirted the kitchen island, coming to prop herself up on the stool next to his. She blew on her coffee before taking a small sip. "I don't think you're afraid of change. I think you're afraid of losing control."

Her words were casual, but they jolted him like a blow to his thorax.

Taking a sip of his own coffee, he barely tasted the flavour, simply buying himself time.

Was Ava right? Was he a control freak? He rubbed at his chest.

"That wasn't meant to give you heartburn."

He flicked a gaze towards her. "It didn't. Well, not exactly. I suppose it's not an angle I'd considered."

"I didn't mean it in a bad way. Only that you've got a tight rein on everything in your life. I don't think it's a bad thing, or unnatural. Given the circumstances. You took on a lot when you lost your father. It's only natural you'd take to a path that gives you control."

Connor rolled that idea around in his mind. It seemed to… fit. Maybe he did always like to control things, his life, his work… "I guess so."

"Take the design, as an example. You said it yourself, that Lucas let you pitch your exact idea, even though at our meeting this past week he pointed out issues he'd already thought of. But you're the one in control of that contract. He knows that's how you like to operate. My coming onboard shook you more than you wanted to admit, not so much because of me, but because of the threat I posed to your control over the project. Every time I suggest something, you immediately discard it. I could see it in your eyes, even if you thought it was a good idea."

"That's… a lot." And not untrue, Connor admitted to himself. Ava had thrown him showing up at the office. Partly because of the Wyatt factor, but more because of her role with Nexbo. Was that why he so readily agreed to not telling Wyatt about her? Because it suited his needs to almost ignore her presence on the project, and suited his feeling of still being in control of the project.

Except was he, still? They'd sent a few updated ideas to Nexbo, and he'd yet to hear anything back on those ideas. He swallowed as acid built in his throat at that thought.

The stress of today had loomed, and he'd been holding onto that idea, and his family's usual procedure that he'd not even noticed his mum had completely changed. Was his trying to control everything back firing?

A hand reached out, taking his and squeezing. The connection soothed his jumbled thoughts.

"Connor, you okay?"

"Maybe you're right. Maybe I have been trying to hold on to control of everything around me. Mum's bombshells yesterday… I think they shook me more than I realised."

He didn't want to mention the design. Something about that still felt too raw. Besides, he was leading the project. Having control over his work was something he *should* have, *right?*

"It sounds as though it's been a long time that the status quo has remained the same. It's normal you would feel thrown. But maybe remember that the changes, this time, are good. You shouldn't feel as though you need to control every aspect of your life. Change can be healthy."

"Speaking from experience?" he queried, letting his eyes drift to hers.

She clutched her coffee in one hand, the other still holding his, and threw him a lopsided smile. "Yes. I'm a big believer that change can help. I think at some point we all crave control and need some things to remain the same." Ava put her cup down, and then touched her earring, a sweet smile tilting her lips. "But there's also always a time to let go and see how that works out too. Roll the dice and see where the cards lay."

Connor didn't know that he'd be able to readily switch up his views. But now that he'd acknowledged his tendency to lean towards ideas and aspects of his life that he could control, maybe he'd be able to work on those. Loosen his tendency to be in charge and only do things he could control.

Speaking of.

"Would you like to come today?" he blurted.

Her hand squeezed his, a knowing look in her eyes. "No. Thank you, but I think today should be about you guys. You should do something different after you visit your dad, just the four of you. I appreciate the offer, though."

His gut churned, coffee hitting his empty stomach. They hadn't quite reached the dinner stage last night, though they had shared some toast around midnight. His mouth twitched at the memory of catching Ava taking a bite of cheese straight from the block. He put the churning down to hunger, even if he got the feeling that wasn't the entire story.

Ava gave his hand one last squeeze, then tugged it away.

They'd said fun. Had he just dipped them away from fun and into serious? He mentally shrugged, physically rolling his shoulders to clear some of this unease. It was just today. It was never a simple day. Visiting his dad was always a knife-edged event. He enjoyed the feeling of being close. Something about seeing his father's name on the headstone gave him a sense his dad was close. Yet forever gone. No more would he counsel Connor or help him with his dreams.

Connor shoved those thoughts away.

* * *

Ava placed the last of her washing into the dryer, hooking a piece of hair away from her face. Connor had left over an hour ago, and ever since she'd been unable to sit still.

They'd agreed on fun, casual, hadn't they? Whenever it suited?

She backtracked over their conversation. Again. Maybe she should have gone with him today.

Dammit, and there she went around on her merry little mental circle again. Second guessing and re-thinking everything she'd said since they'd woken this morning. She wasn't one to rethink a decision once she'd made it. Why was she doing that now?

Being with Connor last night had been everything her fantasies had promised, and more, except this morning she'd been on edge. Connor had looked so… at ease.

And then she'd opened her big fat mouth, saying he had issues with control. What the hell was wrong with her? She was in too deep, that was her problem.

Wasn't that just going to backfire? There was no way Wyatt was going to be pleased to find out his best mate was screwing his sister. Nothing to do with the fact they were related, and everything to do with the fact that Wyatt hated her. How could he not after what she'd done?

No. She would not submit to self-pity. That hadn't ever won her any favours.

Going with Connor today would only have dragged her deeper into his orbit. What Ava needed was to keep things light and fun. They already had the design they needed to sort out. It was a contentious subject at the best of times, and though she'd talked him around on some of her ideas, they had a long way to go before she'd hit her checklist of points that Nexbo had demanded.

Which she *would* do.

No matter that Connor's smile brought her undone, or that one quirk of his grin could melt her on the spot. Her position at work couldn't change. They needed to work together to get this project approved. If she did her job, she'd be just one step closer to what she wanted.

Maybe instead of worrying about Connor, she should spend the day worrying about how she could get Wyatt to listen to her.

Her phone rang, distracting her from watching the washing flop around in the dryer. Collecting it from her back pocket, she frowned when her boss, Gabe, from Nexbo, flashed across her screen.

She swiped the green circle. "Hello."

"Ava. Sorry to call you on a Sunday. But we need to discuss the project."

"Okay. Did you receive my notes from Friday? There is still work to do but—"

He cut her off. "Yes. I got them. But we've just received a heads up that word of the design has leaked. And the fact we plan to level that group of trees that are smack bang in the middle of the area is about to become a hot topic, again."

Ava's stomach sank. She knew what he referred to.

The planned rehabilitation area for the new convention centre was already under fire from various corners. Heck, the demolition of the old centre had caused enough news headlines. Eventually it had been approved, but now there was even more push back. Ava knew Nexbo had been working tirelessly on this project. They were far too invested to see it fail now, which meant they needed to dot I's and cross T's.

Connor's design required a clear expanse of land. Sure, landscaping would be added in around it and new tree's planted. The entire sector was sustainably and ecologically focused, part of her job, but to build what Connor had proposed, those trees had to go.

"Ava, are you still there?"

"Yes, Gabe, of course. Let me guess, if we can make those trees stay, that would work best for all."

The voice on the other end let out a bark. "Well, sure. That would make the problem go away. But how does that work with Gray Designs' vision? None of the versions of the plans I've seen from Connor or Lucas focus on anything other than that entire space being cleared."

Ava gulped audibly, cringing that the sound probably echoed through the phone. "Leave that to me. I'll see if I can talk to them. Just how bad is this issue?"

"From the reports I'm getting, it's a deal breaker. Ava, I understand you've only recently moved to this project, but it's been going on a long time before that. As a business, we simply cannot afford any more hold-ups. Either we get this design completed, one that will receive approval without issues, or we're going to have to look at other options."

Bollocks. "Okay. Thanks, Gabe. I appreciate the heads up. Can you give me at least a week?"

Gabe's sigh down the line was heavy. "I guess I can try. Figured since you were working so closely on the project you'd want to know first. You can have the week, but after that I'll be contacting Lucas and Connor in an official capacity. Let's hope we can smooth this over with no casualties."

Ava hung up. *Other options. Casualties.* The way Gabe had said that didn't leave her with much doubt that the casualties would either be her job, or Connor's design.

And if it was Connor's design to go, she knew it would break his heart.

Ava dressed for battle stations Monday morning, unsure exactly who she was battling or whether it was a more internal issue that she needed the armour against. Connor had messaged her the prior evening, asking if she felt like company. Stomach twisted in knots so complex she'd need a degree to unravel them, she'd replied with a negative. It made her ache to turn him down, but self-preservation had kicked in.

Her fingers had typed and re-typed different responses, explaining her reasons. None of which she'd sent.

She was nervous about seeing Wyatt, but Connor didn't need that reminder. Her boss from Nexbo had called, except she couldn't tell Connor that. He should spend more time with his family after their visit to the grave, except she knew giving him that response was something he already knew. The more reasons she went through for why she couldn't see him, the more she realised she couldn't communicate them to him. Sex with Connor had been amazing, mind-blowingly so, but it also complicated her life in a way she couldn't put into words.

They needed to keep things light and fun. Perhaps now that one night was out of their systems, they could move on. *Yeah, 'cause that's how it had felt Sunday morning.*

Ava nodded to her reflection in the lift's metallic surface, eyes flicking away from the guilt she saw in her own blue depths.

Because that was really why she hadn't jumped at Connor's offer. She was guilty. Of not being completely on Connor's side. Right now, she had to be firmly with the developer, or her chances of keeping any job were going to fly out the window. Never mind showing Gray Designs why she was so good at her job and why they needed to hire her. Gabe had made that pretty clear in his call what her job was.

The doors slid open and she stepped out. Taking her time, she meandered to Connor's office. Her heart skipped when she rounded the last corner and saw him seated at his desk. The indoor plant he'd bought Saturday morning sat on the corner of his desk. A cheerful sprout of green.

She knocked lightly on the doorframe, her heart flipping over another loop as his head popped up, a smile spreading across his features.

"Hey, you." He stood, skirting the desk and coming over to her. Ava ducked away, diving for her own desk and the space it provided them.

"Morning!" Her voice pitched, overly bright. "How was yesterday?"

Connor's brows dipped momentarily. "It was nice. Mum still cried, but they were a sort of happy tears. Hard to explain. It felt lighter than previous years."

Ava tacked a smile into place. "I'm glad. That sounds like progress."

"Yes. It does. Ava, is something wrong?"

She swallowed. "No. I just think maybe we need to keep things professional at work."

Connor nodded, rubbing at his jaw. "Sure. Makes sense. Are you free tonight though? I could cook you dinner?"

More than anything, Ava wanted to dive into Connor's arms and just hide there, but that would not help either of them. "Sure," she said after a beat.

"All right." Connor tapped his fist against the corner of her desk a few times. "I spent a bit of time last night going through the plans and have made some tweaks. Do you want to get started?"

Ava glanced at her watch. What time would Wyatt come into the office? Would he come visit Connor? Her stomach churned and she regretted the second cup of coffee she'd sculled before leaving for work.

"Wait. Connor, we need to talk."

"Is this about Wyatt?"

Her heart skipped. Connor was staring at her, as though he could read every thought she was experiencing. And partly it was about Wyatt, but more importantly, it was about the design. She opened her mouth to say something, to warn Connor about Nexbo's position, but something about the way he was looking at her stopped her.

Would he still look at her that way? Even if she was only the messenger, he was going to be gutted at having to change yet *another* thing about his design. This change wouldn't just be minimal either. The entire structure would need revisiting. She knew his position on changing the structure. It wasn't going to happen.

"I spoke to him yesterday. He's in the office today. At some stage you're going to have to talk to him. I can go see him first though, if that helps? I could ask him to lunch and book a private room somewhere so you two can talk. I'll come with you, be by your side. I know we're on a tight deadline for this design, but I know how important this is to you. I don't want to hide us, this, from him."

Connor perched on the corner of her desk, his expression so earnest and caring. It was enough to bring Ava to the brink of throwing caution to the wind and kissing him.

"I—" her next words caught. *Don't be a coward, Ava, just tell him.*

"Ava?"

Both Ava and Connor spun towards the doorway. *Wyatt.* Tall, hair so dark it was almost black and piercing brown eyes. Just like her mother's. All of Ava's air left her torso, leaving her deflated. She grappled at the desk, looking for something, *anything,* to hold onto. Her time was up. No more diving for cover or pretending otherwise. He'd changed since she'd last seen him. Had she really expected otherwise? It had been years. Many, many years.

"Wyatt." Her voice had an edge to it, the name almost sticking to her tongue. "Hi! How are you?"

Wyatt blinked then quickly shook his head. "How am I? I'm fine, thanks, Ava. How are you?" His nostrils flared and his voice dipped. "Stolen any cars lately?"

She flinched at his words, though she deserved them.

Before she could respond, he continued. "Whilst we're on banal topics, why are you here?"

His sarcasm wasn't lost on her. She swallowed. "I'm working."

"Working." He deadpanned, his gaze swinging with precision to Connor. "With Connor? Since when?"

"Last week. Nexbo hired me to consult on the convention centre project."

"Wyatt—" Connor started, but Ava shook her head at him, offering a weak smile before she turned back to her brother.

"I asked him not to tell you."

Silence met her words, though she could see Wyatt was turning them over in his head. Probably forming an acid-laced reply. His lip curled at one end.

"Why?" Wyatt spat. He shifted his stance, planting his hands on his hips. She'd thought he'd be more vocal, and his quiet was disarming.

His pose threw Ava back into the past. Except all those years ago he'd flung insult after insult at her, calling her out on how she'd supposedly torn apart her chance at a happy family. Her chest ached and her stomach threatened to revisit the meagre piece of buttered toast she'd forced down at breakfast.

"I'm here to do a job and I didn't want our past to interfere with that." Ava swallowed, desperate to find some moisture in her mouth. "I need to talk to you, but now isn't the time."

Wyatt rolled his eyes to the ceiling, his lips twisted in a sneer. "You're sure as hell right now isn't the time. You don't get to dictate to me when we talk after what you did." He took a step into the room, and let out a low snort. "You're lucky I didn't call the police! Dad was beside himself with worry when I called and said you'd taken my car, and then to find it crashed in a ditch… You could have been killed." His eyes pinned her to the spot, the wide-eyed concern mixed with accusation causing Ava's gut ache to deepen. "But worse, you just disappeared. Have you any idea what that did to dad? On top of everything else you'd done, you finish with that pièce de résistance!"

Silence stretched in the room, each word echoing around the small space.

Ava stood, hoping the shift would help ease some tension coursing through her body. Every word Wyatt said was true, but he still didn't have the whole truth. She opened her mouth to speak, but this time Connor beat her to it.

"Wyatt, I know you're angry, but you need to hear Ava out," he spoke in a low tone, also shifting to a standing position.

Wyatt choked. "You're taking her side?"

Connor held his hands up. "I'm not taking anyone's side. I'm just asking you to calm down and listen. You don't have all the facts."

"Right." Sarcasm dripped from Wyatt's tone. "You're asking *me* to calm down. When my estranged sister turns up in my best mate's office, and has been working here for a week." Wyatt took two steps closer, into Connor's personal space. "Why the fuck didn't you say anything? We spoke just yesterday. I asked you how the design was going—hell—you even told me you were working with a sustainability consultant. When I asked how that was, you told me she was a damn legend! You didn't see fit to even mention it then?"

Connor's throat bobbed. He loosened the knotted tie at this neck, tugging it loose. She had to wonder if eight a.m. might be some sort of record for him to ditch his tie?

"You're right. I probably should have told you. But Ava asked me not to."

Wyatt stared at Connor for a few beats, his gaze shifting to Ava. Brown eyes, so dark with heated emotion they almost appeared black, met hers. He looked at each of them, idly oscillating between the two. He huffed at Ava one last time before focusing on Connor. "Some welcome back." Spinning on his heel, Wyatt left the office.

Ava stared at the doorway, her heavy breaths ringing loud in her ears.

"I'll go speak to him." Connor reached out, breaking the spell, and gave her hand a squeeze before he jogged after Wyatt.

Ava hated herself. Hated that she just stood here, feeling weak. Her knees gave out and she slumped into the office chair with a soft thud. It wasn't Connor who should go after Wyatt; it was her. The concern from Wyatt, laced between his acidic words, crippled her. Regret and guilt. Was she destined to feel that always?

To make matters worse, she'd not uttered a single syllable about the threat to Connor's design. How did she break that to him?

Maybe she shouldn't. If she could get him to change the design without having Nexbo's interference, then the problem would go away. Her eyes slammed shut with shame.

She could now add delusional to her bio.

* * *

"Wyatt, wait," Connor shouted, catching his mate at the lift. A few heads turned their way at Connor's raised voice, but thankfully didn't linger.

"I'm pretty busy right now." Wyatt spoke through gritted teeth, his eyes flat as he looked over Connor's shoulder.

"Don't be a dick. You and Ava need to talk. I'm going to organise us a private room at lunch. You need to hear her out."

"No." Wyatt shoved a finger into Connor's chest. "I needed to know she was working here, with my best friend. I needed her not to have been a spoilt brat when we were teens who broke our father's heart by always shunning any attempts he made to bond. I need her to have not written off my bloody car and scare us half to death with what could have happened to her."

"Fine. You're right. I should have told you. Are you happy now? Can we move on to the part where you hear her out? You obviously still care about her or this wouldn't be an issue."

Wyatt sent Connor an impression eye-roll. "Why the hell do you care what Ava has to say? Ten damn years on and *now* you want to get involved?"

The jibe hurt, but Connor rallied, sucking in a deep breath. "You're being an arsehole. You know I was dealing with my own issues back when this all went South."

Wyatt swore under his breath. "I know that." He closed his eyes, grimacing. "I just need a minute to process this. Maybe more than a minute. I'm going to get coffee and something to eat. Come with. Then maybe I can discuss Ava without my blood boiling."

Connor scoffed, amused that Ava and Wyatt were dealing with upheaval in the same fashion. Food.

"I'll just grab my wallet and let Ava know."

Wyatt winced, but then offered a nod.

Ava was hunched over her desk when he walked through the door, her face cradled in the palms of her hands. Concern racketed through his chest at her silhouette. He grabbed his wallet from the top drawer of his desk and then squatted beside her chair, spinning her to face him.

"I'm just going for coffee with Wyatt. I'll make sure you two can talk later this morning. It will be okay." Reaching out, he took her limp hand.

Her eyes flicked to his. "Thank you," she whispered.

"We'll get through this. Wyatt will understand once you tell him everything. I'll bring you back coffee and a cookie." Grinning, he stole a kiss.

Her lips moved with his, as though not wanting to let him go.

"Will you be okay?"

She nodded once, and then more vigorously when he raised an enquiring brow at her. "Go. You need to talk to Wyatt too. I'm sorry I put you in this position."

Connor squeezed her hand again and shook his head, denying her words. "It was my choice to help you and withhold the information from him. I don't regret that. I'll see you later."

Ava looked a little pale, but Connor knew once she'd spoken to Wyatt, it would all be okay. Sure, they'd take some time to patch things up, but he was confident it would be fine.

Then, once that had settled, he could broach the subject that he was falling for her. The weekend had shown him exactly how much she meant to him. He could talk to her, she understood. And what's more, she'd opened up to him. She'd been so honest. Their connection had rocked him a little, but he wanted to see where it could lead.

Wyatt would just have to get on board with that.

Walking back to the lift, he joined his friend. Silence completed the trip to their local café, which Connor broke only once they sat and Wyatt had food before him.

"You know, you and Ava are actually very similar. You both stress eat for one."

Wyatt shoved a quarter of his bacon and egg burger into his mouth, chewing and appearing to mull over Connor's words.

"Lots of people stress eat," he mumbled.

Connor shrugged, sensing Wyatt didn't want to go down the similarity-to-his-sister path right now. "Sure. I guess congratulations are in order."

Wyatt took a minute before his brows rose, and he nodded. "Yeah. Evette."

"You guys good? Engaged life, not what you were expecting?"

"We're fine. Just… Never mind. Let's focus on one issue at a time. I need to call dad and let him know Ava's in town. Seriously, I can't believe you didn't tell me," Wyatt snapped, tearing off a piece of hash brown and shovelling it in.

"I was going to, but then Ava asked me not to. You need to hear her out. I always felt as though there was something going on with her when we were at school, and now I know why."

Wyatt pinned him with a dark look. "She told you? Her mysterious reasons behind her being a total teen cow and her thought process on ruining my car? Ruining our father's wedding? Shit, man, you're asking a lot for me to just calmly sit and hear her out. It's been years. The time for her to come ask forgiveness was back then. I don't need this right now."

"I don't want to tell you, because I think you need to hear it from her, but it has to do with your mum. Ava didn't have all the facts until recently. She needs you to listen."

Wyatt eyed him, his mouth grim. "You're very invested for someone whose only known her a week. You better not be screwing her."

Connor swallowed, his gut twisting. Now was not the time to own up to that truth. He needed Wyatt to listen to Ava, not have him walk off on both of them.

"Just promise you'll listen. If afterwards you're still shitty, you're welcome to leave."

"I thought you guys were on a deadline for the convention centre. Lucas said Nexbo are forcing changes, shouldn't your focus be on your pet project?"

"It is. But Ava is part of that and she needs to talk to you first or she'll be a wreck."

Wyatt shook his head, finishing the last of his breakfast. "Still playing a bloody hero," he muttered. "Fine. I'll meet you at Silvio's. You're paying."

Connor held up his hands in agreement, keeping his smile inside. Finally, Ava and Wyatt could talk, and then he and Ava could get on with the project and see where life took them.

* * *

"I know it doesn't excuse my actions, but I hope it gives you some context as to why I felt that way. Why I did what I did," Ava finished, not daring to look at Wyatt who sat across from her. She picked at the polish on her nails, her stomach churning and mouth dry after spilling her story to her brother.

The morning had been torturous to focus on any work whilst watching the minutes clock over, waiting for the appointed time to meet. Wyatt had barely spoken whilst she'd talked. Connor had given her encouraging nods and smiles, but that had only made her feel worse. He was desperately trying to help her mend her fences with her brother whilst she withheld crucial facts from *him*.

"You're saying dad knows mum was using you all that time to get back at him?" Wyatt said with incredulity.

"I spoke to him last night." Ava sighed. "He said he knew enough, but not enough to make a case against her to gain custody of me. Then I disappeared, and he didn't know what to do. We're going to meet after work on Wednesday. He's invited me over for dinner." Ava twisted her fingers together, then shoved them under her arms to stop the fidgeting. "I'm sure he'd love you there too."

Wyatt shoved his chair away from the table. "What a fucking mess." Ava glanced up, trying to gauge if Wyatt was angry or frustrated. He huffed. "If you'd just talked to me, we could have straightened this out years ago."

Regret twirled through Ava's chest. "I never felt I could," she responded in a small voice.

"Why? I wasn't unapproachable?" Wyatt stared at her. At least he seemed to have calmed from this morning. He was less agitated in his movements. He was hearing her out which was huge. More than she could have hoped for before now.

Ava pondered his words. No, he hadn't been unapproachable, but deep down she had always felt inferior to her brother. There'd been a barrier she hadn't known how to cross. She'd been jealous of the life he'd had, of how easy everything had seemed for him.

But how to explain that to him without seeming like the spoilt brat he'd accused her of being?

Plus her mother had drilled in the knowledge that her brother and father didn't want anything to do with her. A fact she'd never thought to question.

"I'm sorry," she murmured. The apology fell short.

Connor held up a hand. "I don't think anyone can truly lay claim to blame other than your mother. She abused the position she was in, I think we can all agree on that. What's important is that you both know that now. Instead of living in the past, you should look to what you've both gained. A sibling."

Wyatt quirked a brow, shaking his head at Connor. "Who died and made you a counsellor?"

"Just trying to help."

Wyatt paced up and down the room and then came to a standstill, leaning against the back of his chair. "I will not pretend this just wipes the interim years clean. I can see why you'd be angry, but you could have just come and spoken to us instead of acting in a rage. You committed a felony instead of just hearing me out that day." He slapped a palm against the back of the chair. "Communication is key. If you'd told dad and I how angry you were about the lack of money and how you felt, we'd have immediately cleared up the issue. From memory, I told you back when you ruined dad's wedding, but you didn't stay and listen."

Ava snorted. "Put yourself in my shoes for a minute, Wyatt. All Mum ever said to me was 'no, you can't go visit your brother or father. They don't want to see you. They don't like you.' I thought you didn't have time for me. I coped the only way I knew how. I was so angry at life, and everything I'd been through. I know now it was all based on a lie but I didn't know then. I'm sorry I ruined Dad's wedding – he's forgiven me for that. And I'm sorry I ruined your car and caused you grief, but what I'm asking now is for you to understand my point of view. I don't need another lecture on how badly I behaved, I can assure you, I've given myself plenty of those."

Wyatt's mouth pulled into a grim line. "I'm just not sure I can so easily forgive you, even knowing the hand mum played in this. I'm not saying it won't happen, I'm just saying I need time. I can't believe Dad didn't tell me what had been going on. I just thought you were being a spoilt brat."

Wyatt ran a hand through his hair, muttering he had to get back to the office. At the door he paused, half turning back. He eyes found Ava's. "I'll come on Wednesday."

The air Ava held whooshed out, the door clicking closed behind her brother.

"That's not the worst reaction I'd expected," Connor offered. He stood and came around to her side, taking the chair next to hers. "He'll come around."

Ava sucked in a few breaths, hoping Connor was right. A lightness entered her chest at having finally told Wyatt the truth. She didn't know if he'd ever fully forgive her, but then she'd not forgiven herself, so she could understand that.

The project still hung over her head, the issues there only growing deeper. She'd had a lifetime without Wyatt in her life, if he chose not to forgive her, then at least she'd tried.

Connor, she'd only had in her life a week, but somehow she knew if things went south from there, it would hit her a lot harder. She scrunched her eyes tight. Her focus needed to be on her job and its future, not the relationship she'd tumbled into. What the hell was wrong with her?

"Let's go back to the office. I have some emails I need to respond to, then I'll take you back to your place and cook you dinner." Connor pulled her onto his lap.

She curled into a ball, letting herself be held.

14

Wednesday rolled around, and Connor felt as though progress had been made. He'd had a long chat to his mum the night before. They were talking a lot more now, especially about his father and the changes his mum was making to her life. It felt good, as though a latch had been released inside him. His mother had turned a corner, and now he was too.

Letting himself back into Ava's apartment, he juggled the door whilst doing his best to not spill the coffees in the tray he held. He popped them on the counter, tossing her keys next to the tray. He was still a little sweaty and should probably shower, but he couldn't help going back into the bedroom.

Ava shifted, murmuring something in her sleep. Connor stretched out beside her, propping his head up on his elbow and watching her whilst she slept. He'd stayed over again last night, as he had the night prior. He'd sensed Ava had erected a barrier of sorts after their initial night together, but since her talk with Wyatt on Monday, she'd settled again.

Something was missing, though. He suspected something was on her mind that she wasn't sharing with him. He guessed it to be with relation to this evening's dinner with her dad and Wyatt.

Ava let out a soft sigh, shifting again. He ran a finger down her arm, enjoying the silkiness of her skin.

The corners of her mouth lifted. "Morning," she murmured with a drowsy tone.

"Morning. You always look so peaceful when sleeping."

"That's 'cause I'm sleeping." She sniffed. "Is that coffee? Food?"

"Yes, and yes. Coffee and fresh croissants from the café around the corner. I grabbed them on my way back from my run."

Her eyes fluttered open, brows raised. "You should be careful, I could get used to this." Her voice was a little strained, which sent a shudder of unease through his chest.

"Happy to see where it takes us." He placed a quick peck against her bare shoulder, telling his body to ignore the glimpse of heaven that beckoned just beyond that spot. "I'll go set the table."

He moved around her kitchen, already familiar with where she kept everything. It wasn't big, so it made sense it hadn't taken long. He pulled out plates and cutlery, balancing the food on top in one hand, the coffees in the other, and walked out onto her balcony.

Ava was clutching her thin robe together when she appeared. "Thank you. You really didn't need to go to this kind of trouble."

"It was no trouble. Besides, I'm also benefitting."

"True." She took a sip of the coffee before sighing. "Life-force."

"Did Nexbo ever reply to you on the progress we'd made? I thought we'd have heard from them."

Was it his imagination, or did Ava just stiffen? She pushed her chair back from the table, the metal leg scraping the concrete. "I'll just go grab some cheese for my croissant. Do you want anything?"

He shook his head.

Ava returned with a block of cheese and a knife. She cut a few slices off, placing them between the halves of her croissant. Taking a large bite off the end, she chewed slowly, all the while focusing her gaze towards the horizon.

"I heard from them," she mumbled between bites. "They think we're progressing nicely. I, uh, actually have been thinking, about the project."

"Go on." He sipped his coffee, eyeing Ava over the rim of the cup. She was definitely acting odd, stalling over what she wanted to say. "What's on your mind?"

It wasn't as though they never discussed the convention centre outside of the office. It was taking up all their hours whilst there. They needed to solidify the last of the details this week and get the updated model into work to present next week. Maybe Ava was worried about what would happen once the project finished?

He should go see Lucas and Miranda today, gauge their thoughts on Ava staying on in a permanent capacity. She was excellent at her job, there was no doubt about that.

Ava lifted her index finger and chewed on her nail. "I noticed in the files that there's a group of trees on the site that will need to be torn down for your design. I just wondered how you felt about that?"

Connor frowned. "How I feel about the trees being demolished?"

"Hmm." She nodded, taking another bite of her croissant.

"Well… I never like to see trees being chopped down, but we have to. The plan incorporates the planting of more and landscaping the entire space. It will end up with a higher percentage of green space than what's there now. Why do you ask?"

Ava swallowed, her eyes darting to his, then down onto her coffee cup. She twisted it, looking at the design drawn on the paper. "Just curious. Maybe we could go visit the site today?"

"Okay." Connor rubbed his jaw. "We can probably fit that in. I have a few meetings I can't shift, but let's go after lunch. Are you sure everything is okay?"

"Absolutely. Everything's fine."

* * *

Ava sat at her desk, staring at her computer screen, the report before her just a blur of words.

After all that had happened, she thought she'd feel relief. Wyatt was talking to her, mostly, and her father had messaged a few more times. Tonight they'd all have dinner together. How often had she dreamed of having both of them in her life when she was younger? Imagined what life would be like if they *wanted* to be a part of her life? Now that it was a reality, she should feel great. Yet, there was a cloud hovering. Threatening.

With every moment she spent with Connor, she was simply digging herself another hole.

What was it Wyatt said on Monday, that communication was key? If so, why the hell couldn't she be honest with Connor about the project? About Gabe's ultimatum?

Because she still couldn't trust what the fallout would be?

If she didn't change his mind, then it could be detrimental to the project, to her job. If she changed his mind, and that was a big if, then he'd be changing his design. She knew him well enough to know that would not happen easily.

Telling him meant the issue would be forced. No more could she enjoy this limbo of being part of something special. Connor made her feel so damn wanted, and that was all sorts of wrong when she couldn't be honest with him. She didn't want to risk losing him, losing what they had. Would he forgive her if she forced him to change his design?

"Are you ready?" Connor asked, breaking into her thoughts.

"Sure." Collecting her handbag from the bottom drawer of her desk, she slung it over her shoulder. It wouldn't take them long to walk to the site, and Ava hoped that some form of inspiration might strike on the way there. Some miracle to what... persuade Connor to change his design? The design that meant the world to him?

Her stomach roiled, queasiness sitting in its pit like a blob of cement.

Connor reached out and squeezed her hand as they walked to the lift. Ava squeezed back, then pulled away, her turmoil only increasing at the move she was sure was reassuring.

As they walked, Connor spoke of his mum and how they'd been talking a lot more. He seemed relaxed, as though the situation with his mum had been a weight that was now lifted. Their bond only closer, and a part of Ava ached that she'd never have that.

There was no solution to her family situation. Even with Wyatt and her father now talking to her, she'd never have what Connor had with his mother.

She'd never have a mother who loved her unconditionally.

They reached the site that would soon become Sydney's new convention centre. For now, it was just an enormous expanse of grass, work not having started yet. The area was fenced off, and Ava flashed her ID card to be let in through the gate. She walked, heading towards the other end of the site, which was marked out for the centre.

"Those are the trees you mentioned this morning,"

Connor said, pointing to a small crop that sat almost lost amongst the rest of the area. The plans included landscaping, and where they now walked would be beautiful gardens, showcasing some of Australia's finest plants. Sandstone walls would surround the gardens, leading onto what would become a water feature and grassed area for outdoor seating. Ava had read the reports, how the loss of those three trees would be balanced through a row of new trees being planted. At least ten, a range of Sydney red gums, silky oaks and flowering gums, all to be transplanted at a mature stage to encourage growth. They'd been selected, renowned trees of Australia, to bring home that message.

They had thought of everything. Ava honestly didn't know whether the push back that Gabe had spoken of really could be that great?

She couldn't very well voice that position, though. Her position needed to be what Nexbo wanted. And if Gabe said those trees had to stay for Connor's design to be approved, then she had to try. Even if her heart said it was the wrong move.

Dragging in a ragged breath, she started walking closer.

The trees loomed, their presence bringing a sort of unspoken tension between Connor and Ava.

"Why were you asking about them?" He glanced over at her, his brows furrowing.

"I was reading the reports about the initial issues this project faced. The back and forth around getting approval for them to be removed."

"Wyatt did a lot of that leg work for Nexbo. He's one of the best at what he does. There were moments where I wondered if it would go through but Wyatt was always confident."

Ava nodded, her gaze now settled on the trees. She moved closer, running fingers across the scratchy bark. They were beautiful trees, tall and grand, standing alone in their little cluster. It would be a shame to see them go, yet Ava leaned in closer, noticing that the trunk before her featured a fair bit of graffiti on one side. Someone had carved names in the bark. Scrap that, plenty of people had carved their names.

"I've never understood the idea of graffiti. Why people insist on writing their names on public areas to prove they were there."

Connor shrugged. "Me either, but then we all do stupid things in our youth." He sent her a sideways glance.

Ava offered a weak smile in response.

"Sorry, that's probably too soon to joke about."

"I'm not sure it will ever be okay to joke about. I did far more than a bit of graffiti on some trees." Ava gnawed at her lip, worrying one section to the point she worried she'd pierce the skin. "Would you consider keeping the trees?"

Silence stretched, and she could feel Connor's eyes burning a hole against her face. Then he laughed, a touch hysterically.

"You're kidding, right?"

Ava steadied herself before turning to face him. His face was comical, a mixture of disbelief and humour, as though he was leaning towards thinking she was trying to be humorous.

"Just hear me out. Please?"

All humour fled, leaving nothing but a mouth pulled into a flat line and eyes that were now hooded. "Fine." He flicked a hand at the trees, then shoved it into the pocket of his suit pants.

Ava swallowed, willing her heartbeat to slow to a more level beat. "Well, I was just thinking that your design has a lot of sentimental value. These trees would have that to people too, correct? They have been here a long time. Maybe even some are from children. The idea could be incorporated as part of the build. A call out to those who did the carving? We could ask them to share a story about why they were here." Ava cringed internally at her own words. If this was graffiti, it wasn't likely the people responsible would be in a hurry to own up to the fact. But she was clutching at straws here, trying to find any link that might turn Connor's head a little, so he'd maybe even decide he liked the idea.

"Maybe the trees could show how important family and legacy are. They must have been planted years ago. That would only add to your design. The link to how important your father was to you."

The moment she spoke the word 'father' she'd lost Connor. His eyes turned dark, his nose scrunching.

"You want me to consider keeping these trees because you think they speak to a legacy? That it will make my design more relatable because of what happened to my father? Because he died?" Connor's voice was flat, toneless.

Ava didn't know if he was angry or hurt.

But she knew she hadn't made her case well.

He spun on his heel, marching away from the trees and towards the harbour. Ava followed, jogging a little to catch up. She thanked her forethought to have worn sneakers with this trip in mind.

"Connor, stop. I'm not aiming to hurt you, I just thought—"

"Thought what?" he asked, eyes wide as he stopped short and flung back to face her. "Why the hell would you ask me this? Now? I thought we were on the same page with the design, Ava. Wyatt put hours into this project to pave the way to clear this issue, to have those trees removed. He will not want all that work scrapped on a half-baked idea. I understand you're all about sustainable design, and longevity, but the trees replacing those are a better fit for this area. They are more suited to the climate and less likely to attract pests." He shook his head, looking over his shoulder for a moment before focusing back on her. "Not to mention that keeping them shelves my current idea. The space on either side isn't big enough for the convention centre."

Ava wanted to ask about changing the base structure, to maybe mould around the trees or some other delirious idea, but she'd run out of steam. Connor was looking at her like she'd lost her marbles.

Maybe she had.

Either way, she knew that her choices with this project had become far more complicated than mending fences with her brother had been.

* * *

Connor sat at his desk, spinning his chair from one side to the other. After their visit to the site and consequent disturbing chat over the trees, Ava had announced she was going to head home. Apparently, she had a headache and wanted to rest before dinner.

It was plausible, but Connor felt as though Ava was running, from him. From them.

Her questions today had really thrown him. Whilst he'd thought they were on the same page with the design, it was obvious they weren't.

Was this the odd something he'd been sensing?

A knock at the door pulled him away from his musing.

"Hey, wasn't sure you were going to come back to the office after your site meeting." Wyatt pushed away from the doorway and slumped onto the couch. "I quite like this spot for your couch."

"Yeah, me too. I guess I'll need to decide what to do with it once… well, once Ava's contract is up."

"I still haven't forgiven you fully for keeping me in the dark there, man."

"Can we draw a line under that and move on? What good would my telling you have done, anyway? You were on holidays. I didn't do it to piss you off. I made the judgement call that I thought was best for both of you."

Wyatt huffed, but Connor could tell his friend was already over it. He just liked any excuse to stick it to Connor.

"So she's good? At her job, I mean?"

Connor swallowed. His head had darted in another direction with Wyatt's initial words. "One of the best. She knows her stuff. Her suggestions have improved the overall design. I don't regret Nexbo hiring her."

From a personal or work standpoint, but Connor didn't tack that on. He would come clean to Wyatt, but not until he was sure where Ava and he stood. Maybe this was light fun for her? Casual benefits after work?

It didn't feel that way to Connor, though.

A fact he might need to share with her before long.

"Didn't think I'd ever hear you say that about anyone. You're so protective of this design. Ava must really be something if you think she's helped you improve it. Miranda pulled me into her office this morning to ask how I'd feel about them offering Ava a more permanent position on the team."

Connor looked at his friend. Wyatt's poker face was world class, and not a skerrick of his genuine feelings about that statement were on show.

"I see. What did you say?"

"I said I'd have a think on it. I want to know what you think. You're the one who's been working closely with her."

"Ava would be an asset to the company."

"That's it? No other comments? I thought you might have more than that?"

"I think they should hire her. There's not much more that needs to be said, is there?"

"I've done a bit of asking around, her reputation is certainly solid."

Connor spread his palms out. "Like I said, she's the best."

"You seem rather close." Wyatt steepled his fingers together in his lap. "Is there something going on I should know about?"

"Bugger off, Wyatt. Let's go grab a beer to celebrate your upcoming decline into matrimony."

"Decline? No way. Marriage is going to be amazing. No more games, or random hook-ups. Nothing but love and sex on tap."

Connor rolled his eyes, happy the subject had shifted away from Ava and himself.

15

Ava walked into the office on Friday morning with one goal: tell Connor. This was eating her alive, and worse, it was cowardly. She wasn't even giving Connor the chance to consider all the facts.

She'd been scouring the papers daily and had even called Gabe yesterday to find out if the issue had escalated as he'd told her it would. So far nothing had come up, but he still wasn't budging on his stance that the trees should go. Good PR would make for better development. Ava had scoffed at that. Good design makes for a better building, which is what Connor was delivering. But if she said that, she may as well sign her own dismissal.

The lift was especially slow this morning, stopping on random floors with no one getting on. After the third stop, Ava was happy to see an actual person waiting.

Brian Gray offered her a lopsided grin. "Good morning. You're in bright and early."

"I have some emails to see too."

"I'm trying to track down an errant toddler who has decided this is her playground."

Ava laughed. "Uh, good luck with that. She knows how to use an elevator by herself?"

"Not precisely. Miranda is with her, but, apparently, Emily is calling all the shots."

"That's lovely," Ava murmured, ignoring the pang inside her.

The lift reached level twenty-five and Ava hopped out, waving to Brian in farewell. "Good luck with your game."

"Thank you. You're welcome to join us. We're all a big family here."

Ava shook her head, desperately holding her smile in place. "Work beckons".

Her shoes clipped against the polished concrete, taking her away from the lift area. She'd started out this job with such high hopes of obtaining a job here, to be a part of this family. That seemed so far away now.

Dread skittered down her spine.

Either way she looked at it; she lost.

Rounding the last corner, her heart skipped. Connor was already at his desk, an array of breakfast goodies spread out before him.

"Connor?"

"Morning. I figured since you said you had to be in the office early, that maybe you might require sustenance."

It was the final straw. She couldn't do this. She couldn't lie anymore.

"Connor—"

"Nope. Eat something first. I know the past few days have been stressful. Wyatt said Wednesday night was strained. It will take time for you guys to sort out your new dynamic. You've all had more years thinking the worst over knowing the truth."

Cowardly, she walked over and picked up the coffee cup with a L on top.

"I don't deserve you," she whispered.

"You can pay me in kisses." He smirked.

Ava knew he was only joking, they'd said they'd keep it professional in the office, but she hadn't felt Connor's lips against hers since Tuesday night. Wednesday had been harder than she'd expected, and Connor had been busy with his family last night. She hadn't wanted to intrude.

Today she would probably lose any chance of ever kissing him again after she spilled her news. That thought propelled her forward. Dropping the coffee cup back to the table, almost spilling the contents she marched around the desk. And not giving any thought to who might see them, she dropped onto his lap and pulled his head to hers.

His lips pressing hers were heaven, better than the coffee she'd taken a sip of. Kissing Connor made her feel alive and safe. He made her feel wanted, as though she belonged.

He murmured something, but no way was Ava shifting away. She wanted to make this last.

A droplet fell against her lip, the salty tang a dead giveaway.

Connor sprung back. "Ava? What's wrong? You're crying?"

The confusion in his eyes only made her tears fall harder. She slammed her eyes shut and begged her body to shut down, to still this emotional onslaught.

"Kiss me again. Please."

"Ava?" he whispered, his hands cupping her cheeks.

She blinked her eyes open, covering his hands with hers. "Later."

His eyes searched her face. Ava could only imagine what he saw, but coming in and finding he'd done this, it had pulled the last string on her composure. He was kind and caring, and oh so amazing in a million different ways—she didn't deserve him.

He leaned in and kissed her wet cheek, the butterfly light caress so gentle. She shifted, their noses, rubbing before she searched for his lips once more. That contact was something she craved, needed more than anything right now. Needed before she blew it all apart.

"What the actual fuck?"

The words blasted into the room, shattering the spell between Connor and Ava. Her molten limbs froze, each hair lifting to attention, acknowledging the eminent dissolution of everything she'd been trying to juggle. Sick dread threaded through Ava's veins, but she couldn't bring herself to face Wyatt. She stared at Connor's face, his slack jaw and ashen expression.

"You said there wasn't anything going on between you and Ava," Wyatt barked, his voice growing closer.

Connor's chest contracted against hers, a deep-seated sigh blowing past his lips. He stood up, shifting Ava so she stood within his embrace. Something about the way he held her close, protecting her, made her tremble. Even in this situation, he made her feel… perfect. But she wasn't.

"No, I changed the subject. It's new. I didn't want to say anything until Ava and I knew where it was going." Connor rubbed her arm.

"Looked pretty obvious to me where that was going. Your tongue was halfway down her throat." Wyatt planted his fists on his hips, glaring at Connor.

"Don't be a jerk, Wyatt. We're both consenting adults. We don't need your permission."

Ava glanced at Connor, at his locked jaw and set expression. Her gaze swung to Wyatt, his face sporting a similar look.

"I should have said something," she squeaked. "Don't be angry at Connor."

Wyatt swung his glare her way. "Bloody hell, Ava. You've

really come in like the proverbial wrecking ball, haven't you? Of all the guys you could choose. Of all the companies you could have gone and worked for. Why here? Why him? You claim that your youthful poor choices are to be laid at our absent mother's feet, but what about now? You're still making selfish choices."

Ava reeled. "That's unfair. I'm not making a selfish choice. I didn't plan this. I didn't even know who the architect was I'd be working with when I agreed to the contract. My attraction to Connor is one hundred percent real and nothing to do with you."

"Attraction? So it's not even an actual relationship?"

"Stop twisting my words!"

He snorted, shaking his head. "I don't have time to get into this right now, and neither do either of you. Nexbo just called Lucas." He swung his gaze off Ava to focus on Connor. Her body went on high alert, knowing what was coming before her brother spoke the words. "They want you to keep the trees intact in their current location. I offered to come to break the bad news."

Connor's arm dropped from her waist, a frigid wall of ice taking its place. "Keep the trees?" He turned to her, his gaze heavy as it pinned her to the spot. "Ava?"

Her throat bobbled, filling her veins with ice. "He's telling the truth. Nexbo is worried about a potential public relations issue. They've received word from a few sources that suggest there is going to be more backlash on wanting to keep the trees where they are."

"Ava, I'm not adding a crop of trees into the centre of my design. That would completely ruin the whole concept." Waves of vibration flew in the wake of Connor's ground out words.

She gritted her teeth, stealing herself for more backlash. "If you don't, you risk losing the contract."

Connor's mouth gaped. "What?"

"I said, if you don—"

"No, no. I got that bit." His eyes turned bleak. "What aren't you saying? How long have you known about this?"

Ava gulped in air that was in short supply. "Since Sunday. Gabe called me."

Connor's eyes widened, his shoulders slumped as though he'd taken a punch to the gut. "And you didn't think to let me know?"

An ache started in the base of Ava's spine, threatening her composure. "I asked for a week to change your mind because I thought it was better that the information came from me, not Nexbo directly. I'm trying to work with you here, Connor. I don't agree that you should have to work around the trees. We need to find a compromise."

Connor shook his head and let out a soft snort. "Wyatt has been working his arse off to get this project approved. Lucas, Miranda, and the rest of the team here—all of us—have been putting in a bazillion hours to get this through. This is the sort of design that could win us awards."

Ava's heart ached to be so easily discarded from his list, that he didn't see she was trying to help? "So, what? I ignore my job, set aside the directive I've been given, to appease Wyatt's—and your—ego? Nexbo don't believe they can get this design through without keeping those trees, Connor. I don't make that call, the government does. Pandering to your interests won't make that fact disappear. Nexbo are the client, they are the one signing my pay checks. I can't let our personal situation affect that."

It was the wrong thing to say. Connor swore under his breath, his lips flattening. Ava stared at the vein pulsing in the base of his neck, unable to look Connor or Wyatt in the eyes.

"What... you thought because you're screwing me in bed

that you'd be able to screw me at work too? Do I mean anything to you? At all?"

Ava flinched at the harsh words. "Of course you do."

"But not enough to have the courtesy to call me straight away when you find out my design is going up in smoke," Connor hissed, taking a step away from her. He flung his arms wide. "You know what this design means to me. I showed you, when I haven't shown another bloody soul! I can't just add in a different base structure to accommodate some trees. The entire idea would have to change."

Rage and hurt radiated from Connor's every pore. She could feel it like the sun, beating down on her raw skin.

"I understand, Connor. Please… I know what this means, but maybe—"

He scoffed, the sound breaking off Ava's next words.

Wyatt cleared his throat. "I'm going to go. You two clearly have things to hash out, but, Connor, you and I need to chat after you're done." He walked out of the office.

Ava deflated like a balloon with a small pin prick at her side. She traipsed to the couch and flopped down. Connor didn't so much as budge, his eyes pinning her to the spot.

"You say you understand, but I don't think you really do. I've made changes, I've listened to you, all the things you told me if I changed this would be approved, I've done. My father was my most loyal supporter; he and I were so close. This design was *ours*. I have waited years for the perfect project to come along. I worked tirelessly to win over Nexbo and have them choose Gray Designs. This isn't the sort of opportunity that just comes up overnight. Yet you stand there and tell me to change it like it's a flick of your hair or click of your fingers." He locked his jaw, shaking his head a little. "I don't know why I'm bothering with this. You've had no sort of close relationship with your family, so you'll never get it. You'll never understand what this design means to me."

Her heart stilled, the words a sharp slap to her face. She lifted a palm, holding her check as though a phantom hand had sliced the skin there.

She spoke slowly, holding back tears that had erupted. Unbidden, unwanted. "No. I didn't have any close relationship. My father chose my brother. And my mother chose hatred. I was nothing but collateral damage. Thank you so much for that reminder."

How often did she have to swear she'd cried her last tear over her upbringing? Even with the truth now out, she didn't know how she'd ever feel worthy of anyone. This was too much. Being with Connor had been amazing, and wonderful but it was only setting herself up for more hurt and heart ache.

"Ava." He started towards her, regret lurking in those eyes, but it was hard to tell with a view shadowed by tears.

She stood, knowing the waters had broken and wouldn't be stemmed. "I think maybe we both need some space right now. You know what my stance is for the project, but, Connor, it's your design. I know what it means to you, even if you think I don't. If your answer is that the trees have to go, then I'll tell Nexbo."

Seconds ticked over, and Ava desperately tried to stem the tidal wave that continued to seep down her cheeks.

"I can't change it," Connor said at last.

"Then I have my answer."

* * *

Ava placed one foot in front of the next, her gaze following the lines of the pavement with no destination in mind. She needed to call Gabe, to tell him she'd tried and failed. To be brutally honest, she needed to tell him she'd already done the job he'd hired her for, that this last twist was a ridiculous waste of everyone's time. Connor's design was as good as they collectively could make it. Its percentage of sustainable elements met the targets that Ava had originally set herself for the project. If it didn't get through the Department of Planning and other government regulations, then it wasn't from any lack of performance on hers or Connor's behalf.

It wasn't because they needed to take out three trees.

It left Ava feeling as though she had no choice but to tell Gabe the truth. Nexbo *had* to submit the design as it was. Spending more time trying to work around trees that already had approval to be cut down would only waste more money and more time.

If he didn't like that he could fire her.

Hell, maybe she'd just offer her resignation. That seemed like the best answer all around right now.

She'd not taken this job with a view to do anything but her best, and this was her best.

Pulling out her phone, Ava pulled up Gabe's number and hit the green button.

* * *

Connor had spent the past hour sitting at his desk, staring at the final plans for the convention centre. It was a masterful design, of which he knew his dad would be proud. Ava's additions and the extra work they'd done together had taken it to another level.

He couldn't change this. *He couldn't.* However he looked at it, it made no sense to change the structure. To keep those trees would only mean more work for everyone involved. They had the approval to clear them. Did Nexbo really want to spend more money on the chance that it might blow up in their faces? They were *so* close, that matter shouldn't even be a consideration now!

179

He slammed a palm down on his desk, frustration racing through every synapse that flowed inside him.

Shoving away from the desk, he stood up and strode out the door and towards the lifts. Bypassing their silver doors, he pushed on the stairwell door, jogging up the stairs two at a time. Energy coursed through him, counting the floor levels until he reached the top.

Wyatt's door was open, so he walked in, not bothering to stop.

"What can we do to stop this tree issue in its tracks?"

Wyatt eyed him, a scowl pulling his lips tight. "That's what you came to talk about? Not the fact you've been screwing my sister and *lying* about it?"

"Mate, I didn't plan this. Stop being a dickhead."

"I asked you if something was going on, to your face, and you point blank lied to me."

"It's new. Ava and I are both adults. I don't have to tell you everything. Besides I wanted to give you two time to sort out your past. How would my lumping on my budding relationship with your sister help that?"

Wyatt glared at him. "Is it serious? Or just screwing?"

Connor winced, a burning inferno of rage lodged in his chest. If Wyatt had asked him that question this morning he'd have yelled yes. At least for him. Ava… he had no idea how to place her feelings for him after what had just happened.

"Connor?"

He slammed his eyes shut and ground his next words out. "It's serious enough. I can't tell what Ava feels."

"Shit man." Pity laced Wyatt's tone. "Of all the girls. What happened to the code?"

"Screw you, Wyatt. I don't need a lecture from you right now, or your approval. Let's just get through today and then you can punch me in the face or whatever you need to do to get past this. Ava and I are a thing, deal with it."

Wyatt huffed, shaking his head. "I'm going to need another holiday after this." He eyed Connor, his chest deflating after a few tense moments. "I'm not saying I'm okay with this; you and Ava, but maybe with time. I mean, shit, she'd only just turned back up in my life. My dad is over the moon to finally be able to reconnect and move past the crap that went down." He scrunched his nose. "Promise me this is the last of the surprises?"

Connor smirked, knowing Wyatt was already moving past the shock. "I promise. So what can we do about the trees?"

His friend leaned back in his chair, cupping the back of his head with both palms. "There isn't anything to be done. It's a non-issue. Which is what I just got off the phone from telling Gabe at Nexbo."

"And?"

"And he wants a few days to think through the options. The person making the noise has political connections. Apparently he and his son carved their names on the trees. It's a croc of shit if you ask me, but it's got enough backbone to have made Nexbo pause. You know how much they've sunk into this project; they need this next version of the design to be approved so they can begin construction. Political interference is the last thing they need."

"Son of a bitch." Connor flopped into the chair closest to him. "Ava tried to tell me, on Wednesday. She tried to help me understand the position she was in." His stomach roiled, and he understood exactly why Ava had been so up and down since Sunday. She'd been honest with him from the start on what this job meant to her, just as he'd been honest about what the design meant to him. Neither had factored in a personal relationship that had complicated both of their end goals, yet not one ounce of Connor regretted falling for Ava.

Falling for Ava.

His heart flipped, beating faster. He'd fallen for Ava. He couldn't let this be over between them.

"Where is Ava?" Wyatt asked, a brow raised.

"She left. Said she'd go tell Nexbo that keeping the trees would not happen."

Connor steepled his fingers, tapping them against his chin. He had to smooth this issue out, so neither he nor Ava lost. *Of course.* He snapped his fingers.

"What if we use the stumps as artwork in the foyer? The sections that have the carvings on them? They can go in glass cabinets or be coated in varnish. I don't care. Call Gabe. We'll find a local artist who deals with wood, they'll know what to do. The trees are part of the legacy of that space, the building will be the new legacy. They work perfectly together."

Wyatt pursed his lips. "That's actually a brilliant idea."

"One I'd never have thought of without Ava." Connor eyed his best mate, locking his jaw. "I know I should have told you that things between your sister and I weren't just work related. But I meant it when I say it's none of your business. I like her, and I have no intention of backing off just because you now know."

Wyatt nodded. "Okay. You seem different this week. More… relaxed. A bit more like the old Connor."

"You're looking through rose-coloured glasses, mate." He pushed to his feet. "Call Gabe. Tell him our offer. If he still wants our design, that's his only option."

Wyatt cocked a brow but didn't comment. Instead, he lifted his mobile phone and started tapping on the screen. Connor didn't wait to find out what they'd say. He needed to find Ava.

Connor marched out the front door of Gray Designs and turned left. He didn't know if Ava had actually gone to Nexbo's head office to speak to Gabe in person or if she'd just call. All he knew was that he needed to talk to her—they could have their cake and eat it too. His design didn't need to change. She had done her job. The trees would be salvaged, and everyone wins.

Especially him and Ava, as now they could get on with exploring this thing between them.

Walking towards the Quay, Connor's phone vibrated in his pocket. Fishing it out, he read the text message from Wyatt.

Wyatt: Ava had already spoken to Gabe, suggested something similar for the trees. Told them they'd be mad to not go with your design as it stands today. She resigned.

Connor's heart faltered on the last two words. She'd resigned? Why? That meant her contract with Gray's was over. No more seeing her smiling face each time he walked into his office. His chest tightened. No. He wouldn't allow this. He'd fix it.

He tapped out a quick message of thanks to Wyatt, then sent another to Lucas and Miranda, suggesting they offer Ava a job now the contract was done.

He just needed to find her. Where would she go?

Somewhere with food, of that Connor was sure.

Bingo.

He headed for the gelato stand.

It didn't take long to pick out her Auburn hair, her back to him from where she sat on a bench. As he moved closer, she licked a spoon before digging it back into the little cup she held in her hand.

"Let me guess, affogato?" He dropped to the seat beside her.

"Close, I went with salted caramel."

"Tasty. I heard you spoke to Gabe. Seems you and I were on the same wavelength after all. I spoke to Wyatt, who has given Nexbo our position. We're going to keep the pertinent parts of the tree stumps where the carvings are. Make them a feature."

Ava nodded before scraping up another spoonful. She paused before popping it in her mouth. "That's good. Gabe's a smart man, I'm sure he'll jump at that compromise."

"You suggested the same thing to him?"

"Something similar, yes."

"Miranda and Lucas are also pretty smart. They'll jump at the chance of hiring you now I've told them you're a free agent."

She dropped the spoon back into her container. "Connor, I don't need you to save me." Her words were quiet but determined. "You need to stop running around trying to save everyone else. Maybe it's time to look in the mirror to see who might need saving."

Connor reeled, taken aback by her sudden switch. "I'm not trying to save you. That's ridiculous. You're just reverting to your usual prickly self. And what the hell are you going on about with the mirror shit?" He dragged in a breath, trying to calm his heart that had been beating far too fast from the moment Ava had walked out of his office earlier.

"You spend all your time trying to manage other people in your life. I don't need or want your interference."

"Just let me talk to Lucas and Miranda about you staying on. I know you want the job at Gray Designs. You told me what that means to you." Confusion laced his words. What was going on in Ava's head?

"There you go again." She stood, then walked to the closest bin and threw away the rest of her gelato before returning to stand before him. "Stop trying to fix problems for me. I don't need a knight in shining armour. How many times do I have to tell you that before you'll get it?"

"Once more, clearly. Why are you being so obstinate about something I know you want?"

"Because I want it, Connor. *I* want the job. I. Me. I want them to want *me*. Not because someone else asked on my behalf. I don't want your interference. You're wasting so much of your energy on micromanaging people in your life. Your mum, your sisters. Now me. I know what your design means to you, I really do. But you didn't even consider another position. I've had to tread on eggshells with you this entire time. To be honest, Connor, I don't think you've really dealt with the loss of your father."

His head reared back and his veins filled with ice. "I don't micromanage my family; I'm helping them. And of course I've dealt with the loss of my father. He's been gone nearly fourteen years."

"Have you?" She shook her head at him, her eyes pools of sadness. "Sometimes things fail. Sometimes people fail. We aren't all perfect. You can't control everything."

It was as though she reached into his heart and physically ripped it out. He didn't understand how they'd gotten here. Sure, he'd been angry with her for withholding the information about the trees, but that was fine now. They'd given Nexbo a perfect solution. Why was she attacking him?

"Maybe I've been holding on too tight, but I've discussed this with them. I'm not still trying to control everything. Where the hell is this coming from? I was angry earlier, blind-sighted by you not trusting me enough to talk to me, but that's done now. It's sorted. Why are you pushing me away?"

"I'm not." She swallowed. "I think it's better if we end what we have going on. It's been fun, but it's not going anywhere."

Each word was a kick to his gut. Ava was pushing him away, throwing stones and running a mile. But he wasn't going to let her go that easy. He stood, crowding her personal space. He reached out, gripping her hands in his.

"You keep saying you want family, and for someone to choose you. Only you. For no other reason than that you're exactly the person you are right now. Well, I'm right here, Ava. I don't know how many more ways I can show you I want to be with you. I'm *choosing* you." He shifted closer to her, pleading with his eyes.

"Are you? Or are you just trying to control something else in your life? Trying to save someone else." Her eyes skittered from his, her gaze finding a spot on his left shoulder.

Disbelief stole Connor's voice for a few breaths. "Is that really how you see us? Not the connection we have, or where this could lead? Only that I'm trying to 'save' you?"

Ava pressed her lips together and directed her gaze to her feet.

He couldn't believe this. It was as though she didn't want them to work this out. She'd had one foot out the door the whole time. Would anything he'd done be enough?

His body ached, his muscles tense. She squeezed his hands then broke away, taking a physical step back from him.

"I see." Connor's jaw clicked as he drew in a harsh breath.

"I wish you luck with the project, Connor. Your design deserves to be built and shown to the world. Your father would have been proud." Connor wanted to scream at Ava's last words, that he wanted her to be proud of *their* efforts. He wanted her to want *them* to have a chance but it was futile.

* * *

Connor walked away from Ava, and her heart crumbled. She didn't know what to think anymore, only that she was scared.

Kissing Connor this morning and sifting back through everything he'd done for her, she realised she was in far too deep. If she gave him her heart, she'd never get it back.

Could she trust someone that deeply when everyone else in her life had only ever let her down?

Except Connor never let you down.

She flung an arm out, as though questioning the world at large. Spinning on her heel, she walked in the opposite direction to Connor.

She'd done the right thing. Gabe hadn't been pleased when she'd said she was resigning, but it was the right move for her. Ava huffed, wrapping her arms around her middle. If Gray Designs offered her a job now, how would she ever know if it was because they wanted her skills or because

Connor had asked? And could she work there, knowing she'd never really be a proper part of the family?

Her decision to get involved with Connor was categorically certifiable. She never should have let that happen.

Did I really have a choice?

Her body ached just thinking of Connor, of how it felt to be in his arms. She scrunched her eyes tight. No, no matter how much she might think she regretted her decisions around Connor, she knew deep down she'd make the same choice repeatedly. He'd seeped into her heart and threatened everything.

Ava's phone beeped, and she pulled it out of her pants pocket, Brian Gray's name flashing on her screen.

Frowning, she connected the call. "Hello?"

"Ava, sorry to bother you. I just heard on the grapevine that you're a free agent now?"

She cleared her throat a little. "Yes. I resigned from my contract position with Nexbo. It was time for a change."

"I see. Hopefully not too big a change, I hope. We've loved having you as part of our team at Gray's. Actually, that's why I'm calling, I'd like to offer you a permanent position here."

Ava's heart slumped. How often had she hoped to hear those words? Except now she didn't know if she could accept.

"Thank you. But… um—"

"No need to give me an answer now. Take a few days. I'll email you the employment contract and you can look it over. To be honest, your name came up a few months ago on my radar, so when it turned out you were the contractor from Nexbo, I had an inkling you'd be the perfect person to fill the gap in our family."

"Wait, you were considering me for the role before I even started work with Connor?"

"Of course. I might be out of the business, but I've still got my ear to the ground. Lucas came to see me just a few days into the project and said he thought you'd be a perfect fit, too, especially given how easily you'd slotted into the team. We just wanted to get a vibe of how things went with Wyatt, whose praise yesterday sealed the deal. I told them I wanted to be the one to pass on the good news."

Ava felt weak. Not once had any of them mentioned Connor as being the one who'd recommended her.

"So you're not offering me the job because Connor asked you to?"

Brian let out a bark of laughter. "No. He's also spoken highly of your work performance, but we had already decided before that."

"And Wyatt recommended me?"

"Yes. I'm sensing you're surprised by all of this?"

"A little. I didn't know that my chances of a job there had already been discussed before I took the contract, that's all."

"Well, we only hire the best. I'd have thought you knew that by now. I'll send through these papers and you call me next week. It would be great to have you on board for our next project."

"O-okay," Ava stuttered. "Thank you."

Brian hung up, and Ava stood like a mannequin, staring at her phone.

She was a coward. She'd pushed Connor away, all because she thought he was interfering and trying to control her. Her entire existence had always felt as though her mother controlled it. Was that why she'd overreacted with Connor?

That issue clearly wasn't something she'd allowed herself to work through properly, and instead of taking Connor at face value, of allowing him into her heart, she'd pushed him away out of fear.

Fear of the unknown.

Fear of getting hurt.

Fear of being in love and letting someone else in and all that entailed. Could she take that risk?

Part of her ached to just run back to the office, find Connor and never let him go. But she knew she needed time to let this dust settle.

Time to decide what she really wanted in her life.

* * *

Connor couldn't erase Ava's words from his mind. *Control. Saving people. Hero complex. Not having dealt with the death of his dad?*

He shook his head, physically trying to wipe away the mental anguish that swirled around his mind.

Going back to work wasn't an option, he needed to go somewhere else, to talk to someone.

Walking through the front door of the medical centre, he offered a weak smile to his mum.

"Connor? Is everything all right? You're not sick are you?"

Not in the normal sense.

"No. I just thought I'd pop in to see if you were free for lunch?"

"Oh, how lovely? Give me a minute to tell Rhonda I'm popping out for an early lunch today."

They walked to a café around the corner. Connor ordered a burger, which he wasn't really hungry for. Thinking of it only reminded him of Ava.

"What's going on? You've lost your sparkle again. You'd only just found it."

"Do you think I'm controlling?" Connor blurted.

His mum's eyes widened. "Well… yes, a little. You like to be in control of your life, perhaps a little more than most people. But I don't think that's unusual."

"Do you think it's because I haven't dealt with dad's death?"

His mum sighed, a soft smile gracing her features. "If you'd asked me two weeks ago, I'd have said yes. But you've changed in the last few days. You've smiled more, found happiness again. I thought it had something to do with your dad's design finally coming to life, but when you brought Ava home last Saturday, I realised it was her."

"Wait. Dad's design. You know?"

"That your father and you were working on a secret project before he died? Of course I did, honey. He was so proud of you, would still be if he was here today. Not because you're trying to honour his legacy with that design, but because you're the man you are. You're so talented, just like he was. And you're passionate about your work, you care. Those are the things he wanted for you. That's all any parent wants, is to know their child is doing something they love. It's so lovely you're using that design, but, honestly, he wouldn't have cared if it was that or another. I've been worried by how focused on the project you've been, but Ava helped you find a balance I think was missing." His mum reached out and squeezed his hand. "Your dad hoped that by doing that design with you, you'd have something to remember him by. I'm not sure he ever really expected you to build it. He just wanted you to be happy."

One sentence and the noose inside Connor unravelled. A tightness he hadn't known he was even holding on to. He'd thought this design was bringing him closer to his dad, that it was the only way to make him proud, but that wasn't the case. His memories of his dad would always be there, no matter what he did.

Ava was right, he had been controlling everything in his life. Holding on to things so tightly, figuring that was the only way to move forward. But it wasn't.

He couldn't control his life, or others. He couldn't stop bad things from happening again, any more than Ava could control the bad hand life had dealt her as a child.

All he could do was look towards his future. And he wanted Ava to be a part of that future. She made him a better person. Being with her made him feel light and happy. He loved all the ridiculous traits she had.

He loved all of her.

Now he just needed to show her that... Without scaring her away.

1 7

Ava knocked on the door of her father's house. She pulled her bottom lip under her teeth, uncertainty a thick cloud that hovered around her. She'd spent the past week going back and forth on what to do with her life.

One thing had remained clear.

She missed Connor.

Brian's offer of the job at Gray Designs should have made her ecstatic. That's what she'd wanted. It had been her one clear mission. Except she'd wanted it for the wrong reasons. She wanted to feel part of a family, to be wanted for who she was.

But could she ever really feel part of that if she'd not dealt with her issues from the past? She needed to apologise for what she'd done and accept the part she'd played. Wyatt had said she was playing a victim, and maybe he was right. Either way, she needed to face those fears from her past so she could feel worthy of her future.

A future she wanted with Connor.

The door swung inwards, Wyatt standing on the other side. "Hey," he offered, a lop-sided grin in place.

"Hi. I didn't realise you'd be here. Your dad said—"

"*Our* dad. He is your father too, Ava."

She swallowed. That was right. He was her father too. She needed to stop placing those distinctions.

"Come in."

She tripped on her way through the doorway, clutching her handbag.

Wyatt reached out to steady her. "Jeez, Connor said you were a klutz."

"You've spoken to Connor, about me?"

"Yes. I can barely get him to talk about anything else other than you. He's giving you space, apparently he doesn't want to risk you thinking of him in a knight in shining armour fashion, or think he's trying to control the outcome for you both."

Ava smiled at that. Such a Connor thing to do. Not contact her directly, but ensure the message got through from Wyatt. Hearing his message didn't make her freak out inside though, it only gave her warmth that Connor still thought of her.

"Honestly, if you ask me, you two are perfect for each other."

Ava swung towards her brother. "Why do you say that?"

"Because when I mention his name, you light up. And before I went away, Connor was so twisted up in his design he couldn't see straight. I hadn't realised it was because of his dad. I just thought things with his mum had gone downhill again. But he's changed, and that's down to you. He told me everything that happened, about how you've helped him. Not just with the design."

A shimmer of hope spread through Ava at her brother's words. "Is dad here?"

"Yes, in the lounge room."

They walked along the corridor and through to the room Wyatt indicated. Ava felt a hiccup in her chest when her eyes landed on her father. How different would her life have been if he'd been given custody of both her and Wyatt? More to the point, how different would her life have been if she'd just had the courage to speak up, not give in to her fears of rejection.

She needed to stop that cycle.

Before taking a step into the room, Ava forced her words out. "I wanted to come and apologise. Properly. I know I said sorry last week, but I put all the blame at our mother, Vanessa's, feet. And that's not the truth. I could, no *should*, have reached out to you both. Back then. I could have accepted help from Connor, who offered it when we were at school. I've only ever given in to my fear that I'll be rejected, and that's what I need to apologise for."

Her father stood from where he'd been sitting on the couch, then walked towards her until he reached her side. He enveloped her in a hug, holding her tight before pulling away and holding both of her arms.

"You never need to apologise for being afraid. You were only a child. If anyone is to blame for this mess, it's me. I should have fought for custody. I should have tried harder to connect with you. You were only a kid, and I failed as a parent."

Wyatt reached out, putting his arms around his father and Ava. "I think I need to accept some responsibility too. I was too wrapped up in my world to have clearly seen what was going on. I think Connor was the only one who really saw there was an issue."

At the mention of his name, Ava's heart flipped over. Wyatt was right. Connor had reached out to her at numerous times when she was younger, if only just to offer her a ride home from school. But he'd persisted. She'd had a lifetime of pushing people away who were trying to help her and still she was repeating the same pattern.

She was the only one standing in her way of having a family who loved her.

No way was she letting that happen again.

"Maybe it's time to draw a line in the sand and walk past it. What I'd love is to take the chance to enjoy our family, now, without regrets."

Relief flooded every pore of Ava's insides. She finally felt free of her past, free of her fear, and free of the control she'd allowed her mother to hold over her head. It had only taken thirty-odd years to reach this stage of peace with her life. Now she'd make up for lost time.

Wyatt smirked. "Sounds good to me. Besides, I'm going to need you guys around me." He cleared his throat, looking a bit pale all of a sudden. "I'm engaged."

Ava's brows shot up. "What? Wyatt, that's amazing. Congratulations."

"Yeah. I guess it is."

Her brother reached out and pulled her into a hug, the move shifting the last doubts from Ava's mind that she didn't have a family to turn to.

"What's her name?"

"Evette."

"Well, I can't wait to meet her. Since we're sharing good news, I should probably tell you I've accepted a new job. One that's going to keep me in Sydney."

"About bloody time," Wyatt muttered.

Ava walked into the lounge room, her brother's arm slung across her shoulders and her father's hand held tight within her grasp. If she could mend these fences, then it was time to go after the rest of what she wanted in her life. Connor.

* * *

Connor couldn't stop looking for Ava. She'd been at the presentation, not that he'd seen her, but Wyatt had let it slip she was there and that she'd be coming to the celebration afterwards.

Gray Designs had booked out the rooftop bar at the Hilton hotel to celebrate the final approval of the convention centre design with all government bodies. Development would start in the next few weeks, and Nexbo was thrilled.

Connor was, too, but not as much as he was by the news that Ava was going to be joining the team at Gray Designs as the new sustainability consultant. He'd have a chance at seeing her every day. He ached, physically and mentally, hoping she'd decide to give what they had started a chance.

He was letting her make the choice though, refusing to give in to his desire to talk her around or control the outcome. He was letting the chips fall where they might.

Well, mostly. Perhaps he was also using Wyatt's help a little.

He'd been so caught up in trying to not let his life be complicated that he realised he'd stopped living his life. His mum was right. Ava had changed that. She'd swept into his life, a firecracker of complications, and had dismantled every part of the wall he'd been living behind.

A flash of auburn hair set his heart racing. Ava was standing with Miranda and Lucas, her hair swept up into a loose ponytail. Something shiny sparkled at her ears and he couldn't wait to see what crazy earrings she wore. He fingered the box in his pocket, on edge about revealing that gift to her. Her dress was a shimmering silver, coating her delectable curves.

His fingers itched to hold her, touch her.

Surely going and congratulating her wouldn't be constituted as crowding her choice?

He passed Wyatt on his way there. His mate's arm was

about Evette's waist, who appeared to be complaining about something. Wyatt smirked at Connor. Clearly his motives were transparent.

"I wanted to offer my congratulations," Connor said, reaching Ava's side. He drank in the sight of her, her light floral scent seeping into his senses. Her earrings tinkled, little peaches that looked to be made of glitter at her ears. He chuckled.

"What?" she said, raising a knowing brow. "I like the way they sound when I move." She squared her shoulders. "Thank you for the congratulations. And right back at you. I'm glad it all worked out. The convention centre will be amazing."

"More so because of your input. You really took it to another level."

Miranda and Lucas slipped away, leaving him alone with Ava.

Ava tilted her head to the side. "I was just doing my job. Um, whilst I have you though, can we go talk?"

He swallowed, hope flaring in his chest at her request. "Sure. There's a space over there." He pointed to the corner of the deck. The sun was beating down its hot rays, and most had shifted inside to avoid the heat.

Each step Ava took, her earrings tinkled, the soft chime music to his ears.

When they reached the corner, Ava took his hand. "I really am happy for you. That they approved the design. Your dad would be so proud of you, Connor. You should be proud of you."

"Thank you. It feels good. I know my father would have enjoyed this. I know he'd have loved meeting you, someone who challenges me and makes me strive to be better."

Heat bloomed in her cheeks, and it was all Connor could do not to reach out and cup that soft skin.

"I wanted to thank you, for never giving up on me. What

you said that day when I ended things, you were right. You have always shown me you've been there, Connor. I was scared, and I pushed you away. I was wrong."

His heart beat so fast, he wondered if it would explode. She'd opened the door to this conversation, and he couldn't wait any longer to tell her how he felt.

"Ava, you are my best friend's little sister. You should be so far off-limits that you belong on another continent. It's the unspoken rule of brotherhood. Except that's not what I see when I look at you. I don't think it's ever what I've seen."

"Oh." Ava gasped. "What do you see?"

"I see you. I see a woman who speaks her mind, who isn't afraid to tear away my ego when it gets in the way. I see a gorgeous, funny, vibrant woman who eats a cheeseburger with extra cheese plus chips and then asks to see the dessert menu; who loves action flicks and who eats cheese straight from the block because why bother to use a knife, and because you know you're not willing to share; who wears earrings shaped like a bloody peach because you love the tinkling sound they make and the memories they give you." He reached out and sent one of her earrings into a spin. "Who grew up with no one in her corner but deserves the world at her feet." Connor took a step closer, cupping her cheek as he'd wanted to before. "You don't let anyone push you down. You are your own person, and I need you. I want *you*, Ava. Not for your job skills, or anything else, just *you* exactly as you come. You're the first person to come into my life who makes me feel as though everything is going to be okay. That I don't always have to hold everything together for everyone else because you're there holding me together. That's so damn corny, and you know what? I don't care. Because for you I'll go full corny."

She snorted, but Connor couldn't tell if it was from laughter or the start of tears.

"Full corny? Is that even a thing?"

"See. That right there. I'm spilling my bleeding heart on the floor and you're laughing at me, giving it to me straight. You hold me together."

"What, by offending you?" Tears glistened in the corner of her eyes, but from the glow on her face he was pretty sure they were happy tears.

"Yes. Offend away. So long as it's you."

He bent his head and kissed her, not caring that they were in full view of the entire office, and her brother. Complications were messy, but they also made life interesting. Ava made his life interesting, bringing with her full colour and warmth.

Life was chaotic and bad shit happened all the time. He couldn't always be the one to fix everyone's problems, and he sure couldn't control his life or anyone else's.

He needed to step off this precipice and let his father go, instead of holding onto everything so tight to the point he'd stopped really living his life. Ava had said that to him, and he'd pushed back, but it was true. Everything she'd ever said to him was nothing but true. He'd just needed her as his mirror.

She broke away on a soft laugh. "Um, we're at work."

"I don't care. The entire world can know how I feel about you. No way am I hiding those feelings any longer."

"Oh, really? And what might those feelings be?"

Connor shrugged. "I'm pretty sure I love you."

"Pretty sure?" Ava clarified, her eyes alight with amusement.

"Yep."

"Well, keep me posted as to when you *know* for sure."

He shoved a hand into his pocket and pulled out the box hiding there. "This is for you." He held it to her, enjoying the soft O her mouth had formed.

Expressive blue eyes flicked to his, equal parts happiness and question lighting their depths.

She flicked it open and gasped. "You bought me earrings."

"I've heard you like them. One tree and one heart, both made from recycled plastic."

Her grin spread, her head falling back as she broke into laughter. "They are perfect."

"So are you." Connor pulled her into his arms, leaning down to whisper at her ear. "I *know* for sure how I feel. When you're ready and feel the same, you can look under the earrings."

Her eyes flicked to his and held. "I love you too," Ava whispered back. She peeled aside the card the earrings were pinned into, to the key that lay under the soft foam. "It's a key?"

"Yeah. To a house… that I thought you might want to help me design."

"You want us to design a house together?"

"Yes. To signify our new life together."

"You know I'm not going to let you get your own way on everything." Ava grinned. "When do we get started?"

"Tomorrow," Connor said, leaning in and capturing her lips once more. They had better things to do right now.

She shifted her lips a-hair's-breath away from his to whisper, "I love you."

"Not as much as I love you."

Ava was everything he'd not known he'd needed in his life, and he'd make sure she never went another day without feeling completely loved. By him.

The End.

Never miss a new release or give away! Sign up to Jayne's newsletter here to stay in the loop.

And if you loved this book, *please* make this author's day and take a moment to leave a review once you're done.

Thank you!